Amy Cross is the author of more than 200 horror, paranormal, fantasy and thriller novels.

OTHER TITLES
BY AMY CROSS INCLUDE

American Coven
Annie's Room
The Ash House
Asylum
B&B
The Bride of Ashbyrn House
The Cemetery Ghost
The Curse of the Langfords
The Devil, the Witch and the Whore
Devil's Briar
The Disappearance of Lonnie James
Eli's Town
The Farm
The Ghost of Molly Holt
The Ghosts of Lakeforth Hotel
The Girl Who Never Came Back
Haunted
The Haunting of Blackwych Grange
The Haunting of Nelson Street
The House on Fisher Street
The House Where She Died
Out There
Stephen
The Shades
The Soul Auction
Trill

1689

THE HAUNTING OF HADLOW HOUSE BOOK ONE

AMY CROSS

This edition
first published by Blackwych Books Ltd
United Kingdom, 2023

Also available in e-book format.

www.blackwychbooks.com

CONTENTS

1689

PROLOGUE

January 1689...

THE SOUND OF HORSES' hooves rang out through the forest, breaking the silence of a crisp winter morning. Cold air carried the hooves' sound further than normal, as if to alert those animals nearby – large or small, bold or fearful – of a presence. And somewhere further off, toward the edge of a clearing deep in the forest, somebody could be heard hammering a nail.

"This is it," Richard Hadlow said as he pulled on the reins, slowing his horse. His eyes were open wide with anticipation as he saw the small group of men working in the clearing. Some of these men were in the pit that would soon become the house's foundations. "This is where it begins."

Behind him, his new wife Catherine was far less confident on her own horse. Having barely ridden before, she was clinging to the reins for dear life while constantly worrying that she might be about to fall off.

"Just imagine," Richard continued, watching as a couple of the men dragged large timbers across the mud. "In six months' time, perhaps nine at the most, there will stand in this place the most magnificent house you have ever seen."

He glanced over his shoulder and spotted the rather muddy and dirty river that ran past the property.

"Once certain work has been completed, of course," he added, before feeling something crawling on his left hand. Looking down, he saw a solitary ant on his knuckle, and he quickly swatted the intruder away.

"Is that so?" Catherine replied, her voice tense with fear as she still struggled to control her mount.

"You might not think that such a house can be built in such a short period of time," Richard explained, evidently unaware of his wife's discomfort, "but I have employed only the best laborers and -"

Stopping suddenly, he saw that one of the men was stepping on the timbers, spreading mud all across the wood.

"You there!" Richard called out, waving at him. "Mind your boots!"

The man muttered something that suggested he was unhappy, but he obediently stepped off the timbers before turning and grumbling to his co-worker.

"Hadlow House is going to be the talk of the county," Richard continued, still oblivious to his wife's struggles. "Never before in Kent has anyone built a house like this. As you know, I myself have spent a great deal of time with the architect, Mr. Wyndham of Cobblefield, making sure that the plans are perfected. There is not one aspect of the place that has not been given the greatest of thought. And out here, in the wild Kent countryside far from the rabble of the city, we shall be pleased to live most peaceable lives."

He turned to his wife.

"This," he added, "will be a good place to raise children."

"I'm sure, Richard," she murmured, as she adjusted her grip on the reins, trying to get comfortable. "On this cold day, however, I find myself wondering for how much longer we are to be out here." She looked around, but she saw only the bare trees of the forest stretching off in every direction, and in that moment she felt a shiver run through her bones; this shiver was partly caused by the cold morning, and partly by the thought that her husband was building a house so far from civilization. "I rather think that I have need of a proper seat, preferably one next to a roaring fireplace."

"We are here for a very special reason," Richard replied, and now he began to dismount from his horse. "The foundations have been dug, and today the very first brick is to be laid." He stepped over toward the edge of the pit and looked down into the mud where the men were working. "I would not let anybody else in this whole world perform the task," he added with a faint smile. "This is my house. It is to be named after me. I therefore *must* be here for its beginning."

"Yes, of course," Catherine said, looking around once more as she felt the biting air getting even colder, "but I would ask you, my darling, if we can perhaps proceed a little more quickly?"

***

Half an hour later, as Catherine remained on her horse near the edge of the pit, Richard held the first brick out in his right hand and admired it almost as if it possessed some religious quality.

"And now," he said, possibly coming close to the end of his speech, "it gives me great pleasure, before the Lord, to begin the task of building this most wondrous of houses."

Nearby, the workmen glanced at one another, and one or two of them raised skeptical eyebrows.

"Here?" Richard asked, nodding toward the patch of dirt in front of him.

The foreman nodded.

"Here," Richard continued, before crouching down and setting the brick on the ground. He adjusted it a little, then a little more, and then he turned it fully around before placing it down once more. "Or there? You men, tell me where best to place the first brick."

"That seems like a good place, Sir," the foreman replied, with the patient tone of someone who was most likely going to move said brick once his employer was out of sight. "You've done a fine job. Nobody else could have possibly achieved such a feat."

"I know you jest a little," Richard said, staring at the brick with a sense of wonder, "but I wish my connection to this house to be all-encompassing and complete. I believe that any man should be so closely concerned with the very fabric and foundations of his own home. Especially when that home is going to come to bear his own name."

"It's getting even colder," Catherine said, as her horse took a couple of steps closer to the edge of the pit. "Am I imagining it, or is the temperature dropping?"

"Men," Richard continued, turning to the workers as if he had scarcely heard his wife's complaint at all, "is my work here done for this day?"

"Aye, Sir," the foreman told him.

"What are those?" Richard asked, nodding toward some iron bars that had been left sticking up from the ground. "Are they to be part of the new house as well?"

"Aye," the foreman replied. "Mr. Wyndham told us that you want only the best method of construction, Mr. Hadlow, so we're sparing no expense. Why, when this house is finished it'll easily stand the test of time for five hundred years by my reckoning before anyone even has to so much as repair a single brick. Make no mistake, it's going to be a good, solid place and I'm sure people will talk about it for years to come."

"That is music to my ears," Richard told him, and now he was unable to hide a sense of great satisfaction. "What use is a man if he leaves behind nothing of value once his mortal life is done?"

"Richard, this horse is becoming agitated," Catherine said, and indeed the horse had begun to trot around in circles as if spooked by some unseen thing. "I think I'd like to get down now."

"I shall be inspecting your progress myself," Richard told the workers. "Now, I don't mean to intimidate you, I merely want you to know that I take great pride in this project and I hope that you will too. You're going to be part of something rather special, and I hope you'll take that very much to heart."

"We should probably be getting on now, Sir," the foreman explained. "We've got a lot to do if we're ever to have your house built in time."

"Are you sure that these foundations are big enough?" Richard asked, turning and looking around. "I'm no expert, but I'm sure the plans that Mr. Wyndham produced made them look larger somehow."

"We've followed his specifications, and -"

"It just doesn't quite look the right size,"

Richard continued, interrupting the man. "Obviously I don't want to be the type to question your obvious expertise, but might it be worth examining the plans one more time? This really is one of the most important parts of the whole building process, and a mistake now could set everything back by months."

"Sir -"

"I just don't want anything to go wrong," Richard added with a sigh. "This house has to be perfect. Really perfect. And if it isn't, then I'm afraid that all this time and money will have been spent for absolutely nothing. And Mrs. Baxter certainly won't tolerate a smaller kitchen, she already -"

"Richard!" Catherine called out. "Help me!"

Startled, Richard turned and saw that Catherine had entirely lost control of her horse. As the animal bucked and kicked, the poor woman was barely able to stay on at all, and soon she began to slide off on one side. Several of the workmen began to climb up so that they could offer their assistance, only for the horse to whinny as it turned and almost kicked one of them in the head.

"What's wrong with the brute?" Richard murmured, before putting two hands around his mouth and raising his voice. "Catherine!" he shouted. "You must make him understand that you're in charge! Do you hear me? He'll respect your authority more if you're a little harsher with him!"

"Richard, help me!" she gasped, close to tears now as the horse turned first one way and then the other. Various men tried to reach for the reins, but they all failed. "Richard, I'm scared! I want to get down!"

"Will this foolishness never end?" Richard asked, clearly irritated as he took a step forward. "Catherine -"

Before he could finish, she fell down off one side of the horse. Catching her feet in the stirrups, she twisted but managed to pull away, stumbling back on her feet as the horse bucked and turned away. Trying to steady herself, Catherine reached out to either side, but she found nothing she could use for support. Instead, she took a couple more steps back, until she toppled over the edge and fell down into the pit, landing directly on top of the iron bars.

One of the bars pierced her back and then burst out through the front of her belly. Sliding down until she hit the ground, Catherine let out a startled cry as she reached her hands up and took hold of the bar, as if she couldn't understand how it had run straight through her body.

"Richard?" she stammered, trying to get up, only to find that she was impaled. She clutched the protruding bar as if she believed she could simply move it aside, as if she still had no inkling that she was so badly hurt.

"Catherine?" Richard replied, his face white with shock now as he stepped closer and saw the full extent of her injury. "What -"

"Why can't I get up, Richard?" she asked, trying again and again, before removing one hand from the bar and seeing the blood smeared across her palm. She fidgeted for a moment, more annoyed than afraid, although after a few seconds the panic began to show in her eyes.

"Catherine, I -"

"Why can't I get up?" she shouted. "Richard, do something! Richard, I don't understand!"

She tried to twist the iron bar, only to let out a pained gasp as she felt it ripping through her belly.

"Richard, please -"

In that moment, she reached back and felt the bar running into her body.

As her blood soaked into the soil, Catherine's scream rose high into the cold air, filling the space where – soon – there would stand the mighty edifice of Hadlow House.

CHAPTER ONE

AND NINE MONTHS LATER to the day, there *did* stand a house on that exact spot, filling that exact space where the good lady's cry had been heard.

Once complete, Hadlow House made for a very impressive sight. Short and squat, with rather rectangular proportions, the house was in truth not that different from many properties up and down the country. On the front, a set of steps led up to the grand front door, with two large windows on either side; the top floor showed five windows on this aspect, while the gently sloping roof led up to two chimneys, one on either side. With its muddy, dark red bricks, the house stood in stark contrast to the graying trunks of the trees in the forest, and also to the green foliage high above.

As a gentle breeze blew through that forest, the trees swayed gently and rustled. Past one side of the house, a large oak tree stood slightly separate from the rest of the woodland, as if it was the only part of the natural world that was permitted to encroach upon the clearing surrounding the main building. A crude path ran through the forest, briefly running alongside the dirty little river before running all the way to the steps at the front of the house. The front door, meanwhile, was large and heavy, although it rattled slightly in the wind.

Hadlow House was ready, yet at this moment the place stood entirely abandoned and empty.

***

"But not for long," Sir Edward Carstairs said as he sat at his usual table in one of London's more reputable inns. "I don't know when, and with how many men, but I feel sure that the last king will make another attempt to retake the crown."

"He won't have much luck if he does," his companion, Thomas Donarchie, replied knowingly. "Popery won't be tolerated anywhere in this land, and James Stuart will be swiftly turned back if he tries to return from France. There are those who underestimated King William, but I am not one of them."

"And there is another man who should not be underestimated," Carstairs said, looking out the window and watching as a figure approached the door of a house opposite the inn. "You know who that is, do you not?"

"I recognize him from somewhere," Donarchie mused, but for a moment he seemed unable to put a name to the face. "Wait, is it Henry Lumsden?"

"You fool," Carstairs chuckled, "it's Richard Hadlow."

"Who?"

"The dreamer." He turned to his companion. "You must know of Richard Hadlow, everyone in London has been talking about the man of late. He's the fellow who made a great fuss about building his own house down in Kent, with the aim of establishing himself as some sort of gentleman."

"The story rings a bell."

They watched as the door of the house opposite opened and Hadlow made his way inside.

"He took a wife at the end of last year," Carstairs explained, "and then in January of *this* year he made the poor woman accompany him by horse to oversee the laying of the foundation stone.

Now, there are various accounts of what happened next, but some sort of accident befell the woman and she most certainly died out there."

"His wife?

Carstairs nodded.

"That's very unfortunate. And they had been married for only a few months?"

"Do not pity the man too greatly on that count," Carstairs continued. "Now we are in October, and he is already about to marry again."

"He has found another wife so swiftly?"

"And don't think that people have not been talking," Carstairs cautioned him. "The fact is, Hadlow has always dreamed of something he cannot have. He desires a wife and some children of his own, and his own home as well on his own land. The man desires freedom, above all else, and he refuses to accept that he can't get it. Why, while the rest of us are busy concerning ourselves with the affairs of our country, I daresay that Hadlow has barely even noticed that there has been a change on the throne."

"Surely no man can be so insular and blind."

"I wouldn't put it past Hadlow," Carstairs murmured. "Anyway, he has the money to indulge himself in this fantasy, at least for now, and rumor has it that he has indeed found himself a new wife."

He took a swig of ale for a moment. "Let us just hope, for the sake of everyone concerned, that this one lasts a little longer than the first."

***

"Father, I do not *know* this man! How can you expect me to marry him?"

Standing in the cramped, rather overflowing library of Marston House, Richard Hadlow kept his hands behind his back as he forced an uncomfortable smile. He'd been waiting for several minutes now while his host, Josiah Bedford, remonstrated with Rebecca. Evidently the young lady was not entirely happy that she was to be married, although Richard wondered whether she knew that she could be overheard. He certainly believed that no-one of good class would ever be so indiscreet.

"He's a perfectly fine gentleman," Josiah could be heard replying, his voice filled with a sense of frustration. "Rebecca, I cannot find a better match for you."

"Then perhaps you should let me find my own match!" she remonstrated.

"I am your father, and it is incumbent upon me to find you a good husband. Mr. Hadlow has money, and he has recently finished building himself a fine new home just a few hours from London, and -"

"I don't care about any of that," she said, interrupting him.

Richard took a deep breath. He'd been struggling for a while to find a new wife following Catherine's untimely demise, but now he was starting to wonder whether he'd perhaps been a little too eager. Josiah had insisted that his daughter Rebecca would make any man a good home, and that she would be able to give him as many children as he wanted, but now the lady sounded entirely free-spirited and defiant. Richard wanted a wife who would know her place, not one who would cause trouble.

"At least meet him," Josiah said.

"I don't want to."

"You might like him."

"I promise I won't."

"If any -"

"I shall make sure that I won't," she added. "If you force me to marry this man, Father, I shall endeavor to dislike him even if he is the kindest soul who ever drew breath."

"Now I know that you're merely protesting for the sake of it."

"Father -"

"Come on, let us go and meet him. And Rebecca, please... try to make a good first impression."

Suddenly the double doors at the far end of the room swung open, revealing Josiah Bedford with a big, unnatural grin on his face.

"Mr. Hadlow," he said, switching his tone now and sounding much calmer. Or, at least, striving to give that impression. "I'm terribly sorry, my daughter was not quite ready, but she is now. She's very excited to meet you."

"I'm sure," Richard replied, grateful for the older man's lie. "As am I. To meet her, I mean."

Josiah stepped aside, and Richard couldn't deny a sense of anticipation in his chest as he waited for his new bride to make her first appearance. Every aspect of the wedding had been prepared, and as a widower he felt that he was perfectly entitled to hasten to find another wife. He realized after a few seconds that he was holding his breath, and then – just as he was starting to worry that something might be wrong – he saw a young lady step awkwardly and clearly reluctantly into the doorway.

She was, by far, the most beautiful woman Richard Hadlow had ever seen in his life. Petite and with thick dark hair running down to her shoulders, she stared back at him with fearful eyes, as if she felt absolutely terrified.

"Richard Hadlow," Josiah said proudly, "allow me to introduce my daughter Rebecca. She's so very excited to meet you."

"The feeling is mutual," Richard replied, before making his way across the room. Even now, he was noticing more and more aspects of Rebecca's appearance that drew him in, such as her big beautiful brown eyes. "I must confess, when you described her beauty to me, I wondered whether you were perhaps exaggerating a little. As her father you would have been within your rights to do so, yet..."

His voice trailed off, and he realized after a few seconds that he could not look away from such a wondrous creature.

"Yet if anything," he added, "I believe you have understated her appearance. I would be beyond honored to have such a beautiful wife."

"And Rebecca would be more than honored to be your husband," Josiah replied, before turning to his daughter. He waited for a moment, and then he gently nudged her arm. "Wouldn't you, my dear?"

CHAPTER TWO

THE ENTRANCE HALLWAY OF Hadlow House had stood in complete silence for several weeks before, finally, a key was heard scraping in the lock. After a few attempts, the door shuddered slightly before creaking open to reveal a woman silhouetted against the forest outside.

This woman hesitated for a few seconds, staring into the darkness, before turning and looking back across the clearing.

"There's so much dust!" she called out. "Oliver, there's absolutely no way that this house can be ready in time!"

She watched as her husband made his way out from the forest carrying some large twigs and branches, which he threw down onto the forest floor. After stopping for a moment to reach around and touch the small of his back, he set off again, heading toward the bottom of the steps and finally looking up at his wife.

"Come off it, Fanny," he said with a pained smiled. "You'll work your magic just like you've always worked it in the past. When Mr. Hadlow employed you -"

"When Mr. Hadlow employed me," she replied, cutting him off, "he failed to describe the total sum of the work he expected. He told me that the house would merely need to be opened up again, but instead it's going to require a full clean." She let out a tired sigh. "He and his new wife are due in a matter of days," she continued, "and I truly don't know how I'm going to have everything ready for them."

"But you will," Oliver pointed out with a wry smile. "You always do. Meanwhile I must deal with the land, and let me tell you that this place is thoroughly overgrown. There's no -"

Stopping suddenly, he peered at his wife. She waited for him to answer, although after a few seconds she realized that he was looking not *at* her but past her. She turned and followed his gaze, but all she saw was the house's gloomy staircase and a window at the top looking out toward the tops of more trees.

"I'm sorry," Oliver said, shaking his head, "it was nothing. I just thought..."

He sighed, before turning and heading back toward the twigs and branches.

"My eyes are playing tricks on me in my old age," he complained. "I shouldn't grumble too much, though. There are plenty who have it worse. And at least I have some work to be doing, for Mr. Hadlow not only wants the forest cleared a little in the house's vicinity but he also wants me to see what's fouling the river. You're not the only one who has their hands full, Fanny. Not by a long shot."

Fanny opened her mouth to reply to him, before stopping at the last moment. She knew there was no point arguing with her husband, and – besides – she supposed that there was no time for much talking. After glancing briefly at the large oak tree, she turned and stepped into the dusty hallway. She looked up at the top of the staircase, just to reassure herself that her husband had seen nothing untoward, and then she began to make her way through to the pantry while muttering complaints to herself under her breath.

At the top of the stairs, there was no sign of any movement, nor was there even the slightest hint of a breath.

***

The carriage bucked and rumbled over a particularly rough stretch of road, and Richard – after a few hours of silence – turned to look over at his new bride.

"The roads become less smooth once we are out of London," he observed, hoping to perhaps start some conversation to pass the time. "I don't know if you've left London before, but things are a little different out here. Still, the world would be a boring place if everywhere was the same, just as it would be boring if every *person* was the same. Sometimes I think that differences, far from being a cause of separation, can actually unite people."

She turned to him, and he was immediately struck by the glare in her eyes. In the week since they'd met, and the five days since their marriage, Rebecca had barely said two words to him. He'd tried very hard to break through and at least make her laugh once or twice, yet so far she seemed absolutely determined to prove her anger at every moment. Although he understood that she was perhaps not entirely happy about the situation, he couldn't help wishing that she might at least endeavor to make an effort.

"The air is very clear out here," he continued, trying to think of a few more positives. "If you're interested in the natural world, there are several species of -"

"I'm not," she said abruptly.

"I see."

They rode on in silence for a moment longer as Richard tried yet again to think of a pleasant topic. He felt sure that he could win Rebecca around if only he found the right way to her heart, and he told himself that he merely needed to surprise her a little. At the same time, he quickly reminded himself that eventually they would be stopping for the night, and that perhaps at the inn he might have a little more success. After all, the bumping carriage was hardly conducive to any kind of relaxation.

Satisfied that he was correct in this estimation, Richard turned and looked out the window, admiring the beauty of the Kent countryside. He felt sure now that – as soon as they reached the inn – they would get along much better.

***

The door slammed shut in his face with such force that Richard instinctively took a step back.

"I shall be downstairs, then," he said,

hoping that Rebecca might be able to hear him still from inside the room. "If you would like to come down later, I'm sure we could..."

His voice trailed off as he realized that the evening seemed unlikely to go his way. With darkness having fallen outside, he supposed that he must simply find something to eat and then retire for the night, although part of him still clung to the hope – however faint – that he might yet be able to talk Rebecca round. He understood that she might be a little reluctant to start a new life with him so far from her old home, but he felt sure that she must be wise enough to realize that any young woman of marrying age must eventually settle down.

He also knew that his new home could not fail to impress anyone.

"Wait until you see Hadlow House," he said, trying to sound confident. "It's really rather magnificent, even if I say so myself."

He waited, and he felt sure that she must be able to hear him, even if she was not yet predisposed to reply.

"You'll settle in there so very well, I promise," he continued. "Why, I'm sure that many young women would be desperate to have such a beautiful home. It's light and airy, and I've had Mrs. Baxter and her husband go on ahead to open it all up, so you won't have to get straight to work. Did I tell you about the Baxters, by the way? They've been a godsend to me, truly they have, I don't know where I'd be without them. Mrs. Baxter tends to domestic matters and her husband Oliver deals with the garden area. Well, that's how things worked when they were employed by my father, so I'm sure it'll be the same now that..."

His voice trailed off for a moment as he realized that he was straying into potentially uncomfortable territory.

"So you won't have the full set of domestic work to do at all," he added. "Isn't that good? You'll have a lot of time for things like sewing. Do you like sewing, Rebecca? You seem like a very creative and imaginative young lady. If you sew, I would very much like to see the things that you get up to and..."

Again he found himself struggling to finish a sentence, and he worried that he might actually be making things worse. Should he not, he realized now, simply let the poor young lady sleep so that she might be refreshed in the morning?

"I shall be downstairs, then," he said somewhat uncertainly. "I *was* hoping to share the bed with you tonight, but I wonder now whether I should ask if there is another room available.

There's no sense in us crowding one another so soon into our marriage, is there?"

He waited, and after a moment he realized that a faint sound was now breaking the silence. Leaning a little closer to the door, he thought at first that Rebecca might be laughing, but he understood after a few more seconds that she was in fact sobbing. He opened his mouth to call out to her, yet he knew that there was nothing he could say that might set her at ease. She would simply have to come around to his way of thinking and eventually realize that she was actually rather lucky.

"I shall see you in the morning, then," he added, forcing a smile even though he was entirely alone on the inn's landing. "Yes. In the morning. Lovely. I shall look forward to the rest of our journey together."

CHAPTER THREE

"THAT OAK TREE'S NOT looking too good," Oliver Baxter said the following morning as he made his way through to the kitchen at the rear of Hadlow House. "I'm starting to wonder whether it's dying."

Stopping in the doorway, he saw that his wife Fanny was standing at one of the windows and staring out toward the trees. He waited, convinced that she had perhaps simply spotted a fox or some other animal, but he realized after a few seconds that his wife seemingly had no idea that he was even in the room with her. He took a moment to clear his throat, and then – when even this failed to attract any attention – he made sure to walk heavily and loudly as he crossed the room.

"Fanny," he said, before reaching out and touching the side of her arm, "when -"

Letting out a startled gasp, she turned to him.

"I didn't mean to scare you," he told her, although he couldn't help but smile. "You're not usually this jumpy. What's wrong?"

"Nothing," she replied, shaking her head. "It's just that Mr. Hadlow will be here later today, and there's still so much to do. The last thing I want is for his new wife to think that I'm in any way unreliable as a domestic helper."

"No-one in their right mind could ever think that," Oliver told her. "I must admit, though, you've seemed to be not quite your usual self since we got here. Could it be that there's something on your mind?"

He watched her face closely, and he knew his wife well enough to understand that he was getting close to the truth.

"It's this house, isn't it?" he continued. "Fanny, I noticed before that you seemed to become rather fearful whenever this house was mentioned. Don't you remember that I suggested we could look for other positions? Just because we served Mr. Hadlow's father, that doesn't mean we have to always stay with the same family. I can't imagine what you don't like about our present situation, but I'm still willing to consider a move. You must say so soon, however, otherwise matters will become more difficult."

"A move?" she replied, as if the idea was foolishness itself. "We can't possibly move. What possesses you to say such a foolish thing?"

"I'm only trying to help."

"You can help by not getting in my way," she said firmly. "Are you finished outside, or do you have more work to do? Remember, if he's made good time then Mr. Hadlow could be here at any moment."

"I'd better inspect that tree some more," he sighed, turning and heading out of the room. "I only came inside to see if you need any help, but evidently you've got everything under control. I might have to talk to Mr. Hadlow about doing something with the oak tree, though. There's going to come a point at which it's unsafe, and if he's set on having children then obviously..."

He continued talking as he walked away, but his voice drifted off until he could no longer be heard by Fanny in the kitchen. For her part, she'd stopped listening to him long before he'd even left the room, and instead her focus was entirely on the window. She was not, however, looking at the trees outside, or at the garden, or at the gray sky above; instead, she was staring at her own very faint reflection in the glass, and she was watching for any hint that an unseen presence might be watching from over her shoulder.

***

A few miles away, following more silence during breakfast, Richard and Rebecca sat in the bumping, bouncing carriage without speaking.

Every so often Richard spotted something out the window that he thought he might remark upon, yet each time he held back. Truth be told, he was starting to find the awkward one-sidedness of the 'conversations' rather uncomfortable, and he'd begun to wonder whether silence might actually be preferable. At least for now. Once they arrived at the house, however, he felt sure that Rebecca would start to come round.

Spotting a magpie, Richard opened his mouth to pass a comment, but the bird quickly flew out of sight and – anyway – there was no guarantee that Rebecca liked such things at all.

"Is the house big?" she asked suddenly.

He turned to her, and he was immediately struck by the fear in both her eyes and her voice.

"It is," he told her, before correcting himself. "Well, by some standards, at least. There are three bedrooms, which seems more than generous."

"Three bedrooms," she replied softly, before turning to look straight ahead just as the carriage passed over a particularly rough section of the road. "That is good."

"One for us," Richard said, trying to hide the fact that he was gladdened by her words, "and then... I thought I should plan ahead for a family."

He saw her flinch, and while he knew that he had every right to simply demand children soon, he couldn't help but wonder whether a more cooperative approach might be better.

"You *are* of child-bearing age," he pointed out, hoping to cheer her up.

Her lips moved slightly, but no words escaped. She seemed deep in thought, and Richard realized after a few seconds that there was almost an element of panic in her gaze. For a moment, he actually caught himself wondering whether she might out of sheer desperation fling herself from the carriage. He quickly focused, however, on the idea that this type of thinking was completely foolish.

"How far is the house from any neighbors?" she asked.

"I have purchased a large tract of land, so there is no danger of us being interrupted on a day-to-day basic."

He waited for her to smile.

"I thought that would make you feel better," he added. "We can create out own little world at Hadlow House, one in which we are entirely the masters. That way, we can focus on what is really important and we can build our family together. I don't know how much attention you pay to events in the country, Rebecca, but in recent years there has been a great deal of turmoil. My own family has suffered very much during this period, and I believe it is better for a man to keep his family protected from outside events rather than... Well, I believe that a man must look after his family, that is all. I hope that you agree."

"Is there a town or a village nearby?"

"Cobblefield is close."

"Within walking distance?"

"Within ten miles."

"So that would take... four hours, perhaps."

"There really would be no need to undertake such a journey," he told her. "Mr. and Mrs. Baxter will perform most of the necessary tasks, leaving us free to focus on what's truly important."

"Is Cobblefield large?"

"It's a village," he explained. "There cannot be more than three hundred people living there, of that I'm sure. The place would most likely be a culture shock for someone who has grown up in London."

"Three hundred people," she whispered, as if she was in awe of that number. "How can they live so far from the rest of the world? Do they not feel isolated?"

"There is nothing wrong with a little isolation from the chaos of the modern world."

"How do they not lose their minds?"

"I imagine they would ask the same question of those who live in London." He paused, before reaching for her knee and then at the last moment thinking better of the idea; he wanted to touch her, the way that a man *should* touch his wife, but he worried that she might become startled. He kept his hand close to her knee for a few more seconds, and then he pulled back. "You will get used to this new life," he said firmly. "Your father was convinced of that. Why, one day you might even be thankful that you came here."

She turned to him again, and now the fear in her eyes was – if anything – more pronounced than before. In that moment Richard realized that his new wife was looking at him not as a husband or a savior, but more as a kidnapper. He quickly told himself, however, that this was wrong and that he was allowing his imagination to run wild.

Finally, unable to look at her for even a moment longer, he turned his gaze so that he could instead see the passing forest.

"We will be at the house soon," he told Rebecca, convinced now that the sight of Hadlow House would fill her heart with joy. "I rather sense that you will feel a lot better as soon as we are at our new home."

CHAPTER FOUR

JUST A COUPLE OF hours later, Fanny and Oliver Baxter stood outside the front of Hadlow House and watched as the carriage – drawn by two horses – approached the property.

"How old is Mr. Hadlow, again?" Oliver whispered to his wife.

"I believe he is in his thirtieth year."

"And the young bride is..."

"I believe," she continued, speaking through pursed lips, "that she is in her twenty-second year."

"And the previous Mrs. Hadlow -"

"Is this really the time for so many questions?" she snapped as the carriage rumbled ever closer.

"Perhaps not," he admitted.

"When you were working near the tree," she

said, keeping her eyes fixed on the horses, "you didn't disturb anything, did you?"

"Fanny -"

"Were you respectful?"

"I know exactly what you're talking about," he replied, and now he too sounded distinctly uncomfortable, "and I'd like to think you know me better than to ask such a question. I might not agree with what was done, but that doesn't mean I'd..."

His voice trailed off for a moment.

"I'm a man of the Lord," he added. "I would never, *ever* do anything wicked. To be honest, I was too busy trying to swat away all the ants. There must be a nest somewhere nearby."

"Good," she replied, as the carriage stopped and the driver climbed down to open the door on the side. She took a moment to check her dress. "Now make sure that you're smart," she added. "You know that Mr. Hadlow likes us to look our best. He's much like his father in that respect."

"Mr. and Mrs. Baxter," Richard said as soon as he climbed out of the carriage. "It gives me great pleasure to see you again."

"Likewise," Fanny replied, briefly bowing her head slightly. "I trust that your journey was comfortable?"

"As comfortable as it might be," Richard said, taking a few steps forward as the carriage's driver attended to the horses. "Rebecca... Mrs.

Hadlow... will be out shortly," he added. "She is just taking a moment to compose herself." He looked back into the carriage for a few seconds, before heading over to the Baxters with conspicuous haste. "I must inform you," he added, lowering his voice a little, "that she is rather overwhelmed by this change in her circumstances. I am sure she will settle in well, but a period of adjustment might be required first."

"That is only natural," Fanny told him. "She is from London, after all."

"And now here we are in this beautiful, secluded part of Kent," Richard pointed out, as he turned and looked at the garden all around and at the trees further off. "How one could not love this place, I cannot possibly imagine. She will come around soon enough."

"I wanted to talk to you about the oak tree," Oliver told him. "It's rather -"

"Not now," Fanny said firmly, interrupting her husband. "I'm sure Mr. Hadlow is exhausted after his journey down from London. There will be plenty of time later to talk about the house."

"Your wife is quite correct," Richard told Oliver, before looking back at the carriage again and still seeing no sign of Rebecca. He waited for a few more seconds, and then he turned to Oliver again. "I *do* want to get caught up on such matters soon, however," he added. "I did not go to all the trouble of having this house built, only to then not immerse myself in the matter of its daily life. Now that Rebecca is here, I intend to -"

Suddenly the horses both whinnied loudly, and Richard turned just in time to see that they were turning and hurrying away with the carriage still attached. The driver was rushing after them, trying to get them to turn back, but the horses – seemingly terrified by something – were heading back the way they'd just come, although after a moment they veered toward the small river that ran past the property.

"What's going on there?" Richard asks, his voice filled with concern. "Why -"

Before he could finish, the horses turned again, but this time the carriage bucked and began to topple. Before anyone had a chance to react, the entire carriage rolled onto its side and tumbled out of view, crashing down into the dirty river and – in the process – pulling the horses down as well.

"Rebecca!" Richard shouted, rushing across the clearing as the horses panicked and tried desperately to climb out of the water. "Are you okay?"

By the time he reached the river, Richard was in a state of absolute panic. The carriage's driver was still attempting to help the horses in their attempts to clamber out of the water, but the carriage itself was holding them down; the terrified animals were splashing desperately as they pulled and pulled to break free, and Richard had to move around them both before starting to clamber down the river's thick, muddy bank to reach the carriage's open door.

"Rebecca!"

Looking inside, he immediately saw that there was no sign of his wife. As Oliver and Fanny arrived to help, Richard picked his way past the end of the carriage before splashing down into the water, and at that moment he saw that Rebecca was hauling herself to safety on the river's opposite bank. Wading across to join her, Richard found that she was absolutely soaked, and he could only watch with a growing sense of horror as she rolled onto her back and began to cough frantically.

"Are you alright?" he asked, placing a hand on the side of her arm. "Rebecca, talk to me!"

"I was thrown -"

Before she could finish, she started coughing again, trying to bring up some of the dirty water that she'd swallowed. She lunged forward, and Richard put an arm around her and tried to support her as she hacked up more and more dirt and mud. At the same time, searching for any sign of blood, he was relieved to see that there was none so far, although a moment later he spotted what appeared to be some dead birds that had been left to rot close to the water's edge.

"I was thrown clear!" Rebecca gasped once she was finally able to speak. "I was thrown clear out of that thing!"

"Are you injured?" he asked.

"I don't know!" she stammered, as tears ran down her face. "I'm not even sure exactly what happened once I was in the water!"

"Let's get you inside and out of these wet clothes," he replied, getting to his feet and helping her up. "Do you think you can manage?"

Shivering as her soaked dress clung to her body, Rebecca let him keep an arm around her shoulders as they both waded back across the river. Once they reached the opposite bank, they struggled a little to climb up the steep muddy slope until finally Fanny and Oliver were able to grab their hands and haul them the rest of the way. Rebecca quickly slipped and dropped to her knees once she was safe, and she took a moment to cough out more of the river's foul water.

"You'll catch your death," Fanny said, before turning to her husband. "Oliver, make sure that the fire in the master's study is burning as bright as it can for the poor girl!"

"Of course," Oliver murmured, turning and limping away, hurrying as rapidly as he could manage back to the house.

"You'll be quite alright," Fanny said as she slowly helped Rebecca up. "You've had a real shock, and a fright too, but it looks like nothing's broken. I'd rather say that you've been a lucky young lady."

"That water tastes filthy!" Rebecca gasped, before reaching around and touching the back of her head.

"I told Oliver to clean it out," Richard said, somewhat helplessly, as he watched Fanny helping the shivering Rebecca toward the house. "I told him so many times, it's abominably filthy in there, I don't know what can be done but I certainly shan't tolerate it remaining that way for much longer! Don't worry, Rebecca, I'll have it dredged and cleaned as a priority!" He waited for a reply, but she and Fanny were already climbing the steps at the front of the house, and after a moment they disappeared inside. "I promise!" Richard called after them. "It should never have been like this in the first place, but there was so much to do here and I'm sure it was merely missed."

"Can you help me, Sir?" the driver asked, as he struggled in the river with the flailing horses. "I must unfasten them if they're to have a hope!"

"Why did they react that way?" Richard snapped angrily. "Can't you control them?"

"Something spooked them, Sir," the driver replied. "I don't know what. One moment they seemed fine, then they took fright at the same time. It was something over near that big oak tree, perhaps a squirrel or something. Sir, please, they're in such great distress. Can't you come and help me get them free while they can still be saved?"

CHAPTER FIVE

HALF AN HOUR LATER, Richard stood in the study of Hadlow House, staring down at the hearth's roaring fire. In his mind's eye, he was replaying the horror with the carriage over and over again, albeit with subtle changes: each time, he imagined Rebecca suffering a different agonizing death, and he couldn't help but think of her blood soaking deep into the soil all around the house. How deep, he wondered, would that blood get? And what other blood might already be down there?

A moment later, hearing footsteps, he turned just as Fanny stepped into view. He'd known that she was loitering in a nearby room for a while, and that she would check on him eventually. Fanny had been a good worker for his father, and he knew he could trust her with his life.

"She's resting," she explained softly, keeping her voice low. "I think she might be sleeping now. She's changed out of her her wet clothes, which I'll wash, and I put her in..."

She paused for a moment.

"I put her in the bed in the larger of the rooms upstairs," she added cautiously. "The master bedroom. I hope that was the right choice."

"It was," Richard replied, before looking out the window just in time to see that the horses had been able to climb out of the river. "Thank you for your assistance, Mrs. Baxter. I cannot imagine how such an awful thing happened. I wanted everything to be perfect for Rebecca's arrival here at the house."

"It was certainly eventful," she pointed out. "I'm sure she won't forget what happened in a hurry. Still, my old mother used to say that anything that doesn't kill us will only make us that much stronger, and I happen to believe that she was absolutely correct."

Richard opened his mouth to reply, but he hesitated for a moment. Looking out the window again, he watched as the carriage's driver worked to calm the horses while Oliver examined the carriage, and then – as a shudder passed through his body – he looked back into the flames. Once again he found himself imagining such terrible fates that could have befallen his beloved Rebecca, although now one particular fate was manifesting more and more often: he thought of her becoming impaled upon a metal bar, and meeting the same slow death as poor Catherine. He knew he should not dwell upon Catherine's demise, and he'd managed to put the poor woman out of his mind while planning his second wedding, but now she was returning to the surface and she was bringing back all the doubts and fears that had been plaguing him for months.

"I thought it was happening again," he murmured.

"I'm sorry?" Fanny replied.

He blinked, and in that brief fraction of a second he saw Catherine again, impaled on the metal bar as her blood soaked into the ground. A flicker of horror crossed his face; he tried to push the image away, only to find that it came back stronger. He saw the horrified, confused expression on Catherine's face, and somehow he also saw the blood leeching deeper and deeper into the cold, dark soil beneath her body.

"What happened earlier in the year with Catherine, I mean," he continued. "I suppose I had naively assumed that a man could not be so unlucky twice in a row, that he could not lose first one wife and then another, both on their first visits to his new home. Then, when Rebecca was thrown into the water just now, I almost wondered whether there might be some kind of..."

He paused again, as if he couldn't quite bring himself to get the next word out.

"Curse," he added finally.

"How could there be a curse?" Fanny asked. "The house is entirely new."

"My family is not new," he pointed out gravely. "I had been hoping to start the Hadlow line afresh here, but perhaps such things are not possible."

"You should not think like that," she told him. "You are your own man. You are not your father."

"I know, and I admit that it was a foolish consideration," he replied. "Nevertheless, there was a moment today when I thought I was to be made a widow for a second time this year. I have already lost poor Catherine, and I feared I might have lost dear Rebecca as well, and if that had happened..."

"But it did *not* happen," Fanny reminded him.

"I know, but she could so easily have drowned in that foul water, or been crushed by the carriage, or been kicked by one of the horses or -"

"You must not think of that," Fanny said firmly, before stepping over and placing a hand on the side of his arm. "Mr. Hadlow, none of those awful things happened to your wife today. She is sleeping peacefully upstairs, and I am sure that once she wakes she will feel much better. As for the horses and their fright, I must confess that I have never liked such beasts, so it is no surprise to me when they misbehave. That man obviously has no idea how to control them, and if anything tragic had happened today it would have been entirely his fault." She paused, watching his face, waiting for his response. "Please do not think about curses, Mr. Hadlow," she added. "Not after this, not after what happened to your father."

Richard turned to her, as if the mere mention of his father had caused some kind of shock to his system. He seemed to be on the verge of saying something, yet at the last moment he held back.

"You know what I mean," she continued, squeezing his arm gently. "If I might be so bold, Mr. Hadlow, I would suggest that you should focus entirely upon the future now. Forget about the past. All of it. It is gone."

He opened his mouth to reply, but at that moment they both heard a creaking sound coming from above. They looked up, just as the sound returned, followed by the unmistakable sound of a footstep.

"I thought you said she was sleeping?" he said.

"She was," Fanny replied, "but she is perhaps too excited to rest for long."

***

Reaching the top of the stairs, Richard saw that the door to the master bedroom had been left slightly ajar. He made his way over and pushed it open slightly, and finally he was greeted by the sight of his wife sleeping soundly in the bed. He waited, holding his breath, not daring to make a sound at all, and then he stepped back and pulled the door almost shut again.

Turning, he looked across the landing. If Rebecca had been walking around, then she had most certainly returned very quickly to the bed without making any further sound. That seemed unlikely, yet Richard knew that there was nobody else upstairs and that therefore there could be no other culprits. He hesitated, and then he pushed the bedroom door open again and saw that Rebecca had not moved.

He blinked, and for a few seconds it was not Rebecca in the bed at all; instead he saw Catherine, sleeping as she would have slept if she had ever lived long enough to see the house built. Whereas Rebecca was slight with dark hair, Catherine had been a stronger-looking woman with a lighter complexion, and there could certainly be no mistaking one woman for another. For a moment, however, Catherine was most assuredly the woman in the bed, and Richard allowed himself the faintest of smiles as he imagined her living a full and happy life.

He blinked again, and now Rebecca was once more before him.

"Are you awake?" he whispered.

He waited, half expecting her to open her eyes, but the more he stared at her the more he saw that she seemed to be sleeping absolutely deeply and peacefully. In fact, her rest appeared so complete, he immediately knew that it would be wrong to cause any disturbance at all, so he once again pulled the door until it was barely open, and then he stepped back toward the top of the stairs. One of the floorboards creaked beneath the weight of his left foot; he felt a glimmer of irritation, since the house was new and should not have any imperfections, but he quickly reminded himself that there was no benefit to such thoughts. The house was – despite a few small problems here and there – exactly as he had always dreamed.

After looking around one more time, he made his way back down, leaving the landing bare and empty. A moment later he could be heard making his way outside, and then – very slowly – the door to the master bedroom began to once again creak open.

CHAPTER SIX

REBECCA OPENED HER EYES.

She had been awake when Richard was at the door, but she had managed to imitate perfectly the art of sleeping. Even when he'd briefly spoken, she'd been able to remain entirely calm while quietly praying that he would leave her alone. She knew that she would have to speak to him eventually, but after the fuss of the carriage tumbling into the river she felt as if she might be owed a few hours of solitude. The bed was comfortable, she had to admit that, and she just needed a little while to get used to her new surroundings before going downstairs and facing the full truth of her new life.

A moment later she heard the door's hinges groan again, and she realized that somebody was most certainly stepping into the room. She had believed that Richard was downstairs, that he had perhaps gone outside even, yet now she wondered whether he had returned. She could not open her eyes and look up, of course, since to do so would mean revealing that she was awake. Even if the kind housekeeper – Mrs. Baxter, or Mrs. Banford, or something like that? - was the one who had entered the room, Rebecca preferred to maintain the illusion that she was asleep.

She heard soft footsteps moving very slowly around to the other side of the bed.

Whoever was in the room, they were now standing behind her.

When Richard had been in the doorway, Rebecca had risked opening her eyes very slightly, just enough so that she had been able to peep and see him. She felt sure that he had not realized. Now, however, she knew that this new visitor was much closer, and that her efforts to appear to be sleeping needed to be much more authentic. She wondered why anyone would enter the room and simply stand behind her, but a moment later she had to stop herself flinching as the bed shifted slightly and she felt the weight of somebody sitting behind her.

"Why?"

"Why can't I be left alone?" she thought. "Please, is that too much to ask?"

She swallowed hard, but she kept her eyes

shut. If Richard had indeed returned to the room, she could only hope that he might leave soon; if Mrs. Baxter was the visitor, then she assumed the older woman was simply checking on her health. As the seconds passed, however, Rebecca began to feel distinctly uneasy, until suddenly she felt a hand touching her shoulder from behind. She managed – again – not to flinch, but now she couldn't help noticing that this hand seemed very cold, and indeed that the air all around her in the room was growing an icy edge. Swallowing again, Rebecca prayed for the hand to move away, yet it lingered and continued to rest on her shoulder for several seconds.

"Mr. Baxter!" Richard called out from outside. "Might you help me with this?"

Rebecca felt a flush of relief. At least this meant that her visitor must be the housekeeper.

"Oliver is around the other side of the house," Mrs. Baxter's voice said suddenly, and she too was clearly outside. "I shall fetch him at once."

Opening her eyes, Rebecca realized that somebody else must be in the room with her. For a moment she was too shocked to move, and then – wondering whether she had misunderstood the make-up of the household – she sat up and turned to look over her shoulder, at which point she felt the hand fade away. She opened her mouth to speak, only to let out a faint gasp as she found instead that there was now nobody else with her in the room at all.

***

"There you are," Fanny said, glancing across the kitchen with a smile as soon as Rebecca reached the doorway a few minutes later. "I had thought you might rest for a little while longer."

Rebecca watched for a few seconds as Fanny worked the flour on the counter-top.

"You can sit with me if you prefer," Fanny continued. "Mr. Hadlow is outside, directing my husband in the commission of some work that suddenly struck them both as being hugely important. I confess that I do not know precisely what."

"And what of the other?" Rebecca asked.

"Other?"

"Who else is here?" Rebecca continued, looking around. "There is another, is there not?"

"I am not sure what you mean," Fanny replied cautiously.

"Well, I -"

Rebecca hesitated, but at that moment she realized that she had perhaps been dreaming. After all, there was no way that anyone could have left the master bedroom so swiftly, and anyway... the hand had felt less solid as it had pulled away from her shoulder and more like it had simply blinked out of existence. Still, she could not help but look over her shoulder and watch the gloomy hallway for a moment, before turning to once again watch Fanny at work.

"How do you feel now?" Fanny asked. "You must at least have a few aches and bruises after your fall into the river."

"I think not," Rebecca said, reaching up and touching the side of her neck. "Some stiffness, perhaps, but otherwise I appear to have emerged miraculously unscathed."

"For that, we must all be thankful."

After hesitating for a moment, Rebecca made her way over to the table in the corner. She looked down at the various herbs and plants that Fanny had laid out to dry, and she realized that she had no idea what any of these things might be. Indeed, the more she looked around the kitchen, the more she felt lost in a world of alien things. Her father had tried to teach her about cooking and housekeeping, of course, but she still felt woefully under-prepared to take on any kind of duty, and she realized that soon everyone would realize that she was an impostor. Richard Hadlow thought that he had married and acquired a new wife, yet Rebecca knew deep down that she was unable to take on any of the roles that might be reasonably expected of her.

She turned to Fanny and almost asked for help, before deciding at the last second that this would be a mistake. Instead, she supposed that she would have to try to learn fast.

"There was another Mrs. Hadlow, was there not?" she said cautiously.

"Do you know much about cooking?" Fanny asked.

"Richard was married before, and I believe it was only this year too. Who was -"

"I can teach you," Fanny added, interrupting her this time. "I'm sure you feel rather lost."

"There was another wife," Rebecca replied. "She lived here, I must assume. I know that she died, but I confess I do not know the details of -"

"You will need to be a fast learner," Fanny told her, cutting her off yet again. "All woman must. We'll soon have you up and running, though."

"Please, Mrs. Baker -"

"Baxter, my dear. My name is Mrs. Baxter."

"Mrs. Baxter, what happened to Mr. Hadlow's first wife?"

"If -"

"How did she die? What -"

Suddenly Fanny turned to her, and for a moment the older woman's eyes were filled with rage. After a few seconds, Rebecca looked down and saw the kitchen knife she was holding in her right hand.

"There is a time and a place for such questions," Fanny said, sounding a little panicked and breathless now. She took a moment to calm herself down a little. "This is not that time," she added, "or that place. Some things are best left in the past, and you really must try to focus on the task at hand, which is to become the best possible wife for Master Hadlow." She paused for a few seconds. "He really *is* a good man, you know," she added. "You mustn't let foolish thoughts fill your head. Instead you must thank the Lord that you have been given this wonderful opportunity and you must get to work trying to become the best possible wife. Do you think you can do that?"

Rebecca hesitated, although she was fully aware that there was only one correct answer to that question. The moment had arrived for her to accept her fate.

"Yes," she said finally, before resolving to sound a little more determined. "Yes," she said again. "Indeed."

"Then let me guide you," Fanny replied, before stepping over to the table. Still holding the knife, she used its tip to indicate a large collection of dark green leaves. "Do you know what this is?"

"I confess, I do not," Rebecca told her hopelessly.

"Then I shall educate you, my dear," Fanny said with a faint smile. "There's a lot for you to learn here, however, so I hope you'll pay very strict attention."

CHAPTER SEVEN

"IT'S GOING TO BE a full week's work, Sir," Oliver said as he stood out at the end of the garden, looking down into the sludgy, unwelcoming sight of the river. "Perhaps two, even."

"That's as may be," Richard replied, "but it must be done. I trust that you have all the tools you require?"

"There aren't many tools that'll be involved," Oliver muttered. "It's going to be brute strength that's required."

"Do you need some help? I would most certainly be happy to offer any assistance that you might need."

"That's very kind of you, Sir," Oliver said, "but in truth, I work better on my own, and I think I'd rather be left to get on with it." He pointed toward a particularly large pile of mud on the river's other side. "My first job'll be to clear that part and get rid of all the weeds. The wheels of that carriage churned a lot of dirt up."

"At least the wretched fellow is gone now," Richard said with a sigh. "And he took his horses with him."

"The carriage wasn't actually damaged too much," Oliver explained. "This'll be a hard job, but I have no doubt whatsoever that it can be done."

"And what is this?" Richard asked, stepping past him and then crouching down to get a better view of what appeared to be a rotten dead bird just above the water line, with thick maggots crawling through its guts. "Would you mind removing anything like this first, Oliver? I should not like my wife to see so much death."

"Of course."

Heading over, Oliver reached down and picked up the dead bird with his bare hands. As soon as he lifted the main part of the corpse up, the head slithered off and hung down, attached to the main part of the body by a thin strand of meat. Clearly untroubled by such things, Oliver scooped the rest of the bird up – maggots and all – and peered more closely at the remains, before sniffing the air slightly.

"It smells bad, that's for sure," he said.

"Are you sure that it's wise to hold that thing

in such a manner?" Richard asked, wincing a little as he saw that one of the maggots was now crawling off the dead bird and along Oliver's hand, heading up onto the man's wrist. "I must say, it's all rather horrible."

"I'll bury it," Oliver replied, before turning and chucking the rotten dead bird down onto the ground with force. Turning back to Richard, he smiled. "It'll be good for the soil."

"I'm sure," Richard said, and then he winced again as he saw that the stray maggot was still crawling across Oliver's wrist, making its way up into the sleeve of his tunic. "Oliver, you have..."

His voice trailed off as the maggot disappeared from view.

"Oh?" Oliver looked down, pulled the tunic's sleeve aside, and then flicked the maggot away. "Don't mind things like that too much, Sir. Out here in the countryside, you'll never be too far from something like that."

"Evidently," Richard said, with no obvious sign of pleasure. "Still, there seems to be no need to actively invite these creatures to come too close."

"I'll dig out anything that's down in that riverbed," Oliver explained, "and clear the weeds, and then I reckon that within a week or two the water'll flow more cleanly. There's only so much I can manage, of course, because a lot depends on whatever's going on upstream, but I'm sure we can at least improve things a little. That's about all I can promise, though."

"I'm sure you'll do your best," Richard said, forcing a smile. "Thank you, Oliver. I trust that you recognize my gratitude for all that you and your wife have done for me."

"We served your father," Oliver said firmly, "and now we serve you." He paused for a few more seconds. "Although I do find myself wondering how long you might want us around, Sir. If you ever come to think that we're surplus to requirements, I would ask that you give us plenty of warning. Fanny and I are still young enough to find other work, just about, but we'd need as much time as possible. If you catch my drift."

"I do," Richard told him, "and -"

Stopping suddenly, he turned and looked across the garden. For a few seconds his eyes searched for something, and then – as a faint scratching sound briefly filled the air – he found himself staring at the old oak tree.

"I've been meaning to talk to you about that thing, Sir," Oliver continued. "It's not looking healthy, and in my experience it's better to get the remedial action in sooner rather than later. If I cut off some branches now, we might be able to save the thing, otherwise it'll become too dangerous to let it stand. Obviously it's a big job and it'll have to wait until after I've done the river, but it's not something that can really be put off."

"Of course," Richard replied, still watching the tree and then – turning his head a little – staring toward the patch of ground between the gnarled roots and the forest's clearing. "Did you hear something a moment ago?" he continued, his voice filled now with a sense of wonder. "Like a kind of... scratching sound?"

"You'll hear all sorts out here," Oliver told him. "In my experience, it's best not to think about such things too much, otherwise you can find your imagination runs wild. Trust me, Sir. Let me look after the outside. You've got your nice young wife to take care of now."

***

A few minutes later, as he set some old saws against the wall around the rear of the house, Oliver heard the back door open. Looking up, he saw Fanny stepping outside.

"How are things in there?" he asked. "Have you trained her up to become the perfect wife yet?"

"She's very rough around the edges," Fanny replied, glancing back to make sure that she couldn't be overheard, before pushing the door shut and making her way over to join her husband, "but not without potential. As long as she truly *wants* to learn, she'll be fine."

"Doesn't seem to me as if she'll have much choice," he observed.

"And what has the master got you doing now?" she asked, stopping and looking at the rusty metal teeth of the saws. "Those things look like they're left from the days of Queen Elizabeth herself."

"You might not be too wrong there," he muttered, taking a step back. He paused, looking at the saws, before turning to his wife. "Mr. Hadlow seemed drawn to the spot next to the tree a little earlier"

"What spot next to the tree?"

"You know full well what I'm talking about."

"Let him go," she replied. "It's no concern of ours."

"I just think it'd be a good idea to keep him away."

"He knows what's there," she pointed out. "He can go rooting around in the undergrowth as much as he wants, he'll only find things that he already knows about."

"Yes, but -"

"Do not start talking to me again about things that cannot be real, Oliver," she said firmly. "I'm sorry, I did not mean to speak over you, but I will not have any more talk of... such things."

"It was like he heard something," he told

her. "He said as much himself. He mentioned a scratching sound, and I too have heard a -"

"You have heard nothing of the sort," she said through gritted teeth. "Oliver, you are a good man, and I will not have you dredging up the past in this manner. Not when you already have a perfectly good river that needs dredging. Do you understand? There is no -"

Before she could finish, they both heard Rebecca laughing inside the house.

"I told her to show Mr. Hadlow what we're making for this evening's meal," she continued, "and I don't know about you, but I certainly think that they seem to be getting on very well now. Please, let us not do anything that risks pushing them apart again. We've talked about this before, Oliver. We both know that after everything he has endured in recent years, Mr. Hadlow is more deserving than almost any other man of a fresh start. And I for one intend to do everything in my power to make sure that he gets one."

She wiped her hands on the sides of her apron, before turning and heading back into the house.

"I trust," she added, "that you won't do anything foolish."

"Oh, I'll keep my mouth shut," he sighed once she was gone. "I know better than to cause trouble."

As he heard Rebecca laughing again, Oliver picked up the largest of the saws and began to examine the sharp little metal teeth. Having sat for a long time without being maintained, this saw was one of the rustier specimens, and when he touched some of the teeth Oliver winced as he felt a pinprick of pain. Still, as he peered more closely at the saw's leading edge, he reasoned that there was no need to throw any of the saws out; when the time came, they would all most likely still be capable of cutting through anything in their way.

CHAPTER EIGHT

"A MAN IS NEVER happier than when his belly is full," Richard said a few hours later, as he stood in the house's study with several candles burning nearby, "and I contend that my belly is very full right now."

"Mrs. Baxter did all the hard work," Rebecca replied cautiously, watching him from the doorway from a moment. "Indeed, I should go and help her clean up."

She turned to leave the room.

"No, wait!" Richard said abruptly.

Stopping, Rebecca turned to him.

"Let us be honest with one another," he continued. "Our journey here was uncomfortable, to say the least. I'm not saying that you set out to be deliberately cold or rude, but your displeasure with the whole arrangement was plain to see and – I might add – entirely understandable. As for my part, I tried to make you feel better, but I did a very bad job of that and I confess I think I might have made things worse. I hope you'll understand that my efforts were ruined, if anything, by an overeager desire to please you."

"You have been most kind since the moment we first met," she told him.

"This cannot be easy for you," he replied. "You are in a strange house in a strange place, with a strange housekeeper and a strange groundsman, working in a strange kitchen and dealing with..." He paused. "A strange husband."

"You have been most kind," she said again.

"I want to turn this place into a home," he explained. "I don't know how much your father told you about my family, but in recent years the Hadlows have... been on the wrong side of history. My forebears picked the losing side in the fight for the nation forty years ago, and they picked the losing side again in recent years when the last king made his play to bring back the cursed religion. Speak to anyone in circles of power in this country, and they will most likely spit whenever they heard the name Hadlow."

"I am sure things aren't that bad."

"Oh, but they are," he told her, before allowing himself a faint smile. "They truly are. And if I might be so bold, I believe myself to be the first Hadlow in quite some time who has not gone out of his way to appear a fool in front of the authorities. I am still stained by the actions of my father and grandfather, and of several generations before that, but I am resolved to break free from that litany of foolishness and stand on my own two feet. That is why I wanted to have a new house built, one that has no... history."

"I can understand that," she replied meekly, although she still seemed keen to leave the room.

"A new house," he continued, "and a wife, and hopefully soon some children to fill the empty spaces."

At this, Rebecca lowered her gaze a little.

"These things will take time," Richard told her, before making his way across the room and stopping to look down at her face, "but I am a patient man. And I hope that, even if you feel no love for me now, you will at least remain open to the possibility that you might one day tolerate my company.

"You are a kind man," she replied, looking up at him again, and now she was blushing a little. "I should have been more convivial when we first met, and during our journey down here, and for that I can only apologize."

"No apology is necessary."

"It is," she said firmly, "and you know as

much. I think my young age robs me of the necessary maturity at times, but I shall endeavor to find a way to please you better." She paused again, staring into his eyes, and she stayed close to him even though her instincts told her to move back a little. "I still have so much to learn," she added, and now her voice was trembling a little with fear, "but with your good grace and a little patience, I hope to become the sort of wife that you desire."

"I'm sure you will," he told her. "You have already tested the marital bed. I hope you found it to your satisfaction."

"I did," she said, and she was starting to wonder whether she might be blushing.

For the next few seconds, an awkward silence fell between them once more, but this was not the same as the silence in the carriage. This time the silence seemed to be fill with a kind of nervous anticipation, and Rebecca told herself that – as the wife – she had to wait and follow her husband's cue. In truth, she had never felt so hopelessly naive and inexperienced as she felt at that moment, and she desperately wanted Richard to take the lead. With each second that passed, however, she began to wonder whether she was doing something wrong, whether she perhaps should be the one to show some initiative.

And then, just as she was trying to think of some other move, Richard reached out and put his hands on the side of her face, and then he leaned close and pressed his closed mouth against hers.

Startled, but supposing this must be a kiss, Rebecca waited. She had never been kissed before and had never even seen anyone kissing, save for some decorous pecks on the cheeks of a few relatives now and again, but she assumed that a kiss between a husband and a wife must be different in some way. Nevertheless, Richard kept his mouth firmly shut, while the whiskers of his upper lip ticked her face. After a few seconds, supposing that she should make a move, Rebecca opened her mouth and moved her tongue close to her own teeth, but Richard did not reciprocate and instead he merely pressed his face harder against hers until their open eyes were mere fractions of an inch apart.

Finally, after what felt like an eternity, Richard pulled back. Rebecca, completely confused by what had just happened, realized that now she was *definitely* blushing.

"Well," Richard said, forcing a smile, "now we have had our first kiss."

"Yes," she replied demurely, supposing that she must have simply misunderstood how kissing worked. "It was good to do that."

"We shall do it some more," he told her, "although now I feel that the hour is getting late and we must both prepare for bed. Please check with Mrs. Baxter and see whether she requires anything else from you, and then I shall see you in the bedchamber."

"Of course," she said, trying not to appear flustered as she turned and hurried out of the room. "I'm sorry. I should have done that already. Please forgive me."

***

A short while later, having assisted Mrs. Baxter in the discharge of certain duties in the kitchen and pantry, Rebecca made her way up the stairs. She had been dreading this moment somewhat, worried that her wifely duties in the bedroom might prove rather difficult and awkward, but she knew she could delay no longer. Richard was already in the master bedroom, no doubt waiting for her arrival.

Reaching the top of the stairs, she hesitated for a moment. The kiss earlier had certainly been unlike anything she had anticipated, and now her mind was racing as she began to wonder what might be about to happen next. She had heard only a few fleeting whispers over the years about copulation, and she felt that her twenty-two years of life so far had left her woefully unprepared for this moment. Indeed, she worried that she was bound to disappoint her husband, although she quickly reminded herself that he would most likely take the lead.

After all, he had known how to kiss.

As she stepped forward, she happened to glance out the window, and she immediately froze as soon as she spotted a figure standing next to the old oak tree. Puzzled, she squinted a little in an attempt to see better; she could tell that the figure was a woman wearing a white dress, although the garden was very dark and she was unable to make out many details. The woman seemed to have quite light hair, and after a few seconds Rebecca felt a shiver pass through her chest as she realized that this was most certainly not Mrs. Baxter. Whoever was out there, she appeared to be staring directly up at Rebecca, almost as if – even from a couple of hundred feet away – she had anticipated her arrival at the window.

Rebecca opened her mouth to wonder out loud who might be in the garden, but at that moment she heard a bump coming from the master bedroom. She turned and looked at the half-open door, and then she looked out the window again, only to find that this time the strange woman was nowhere to be seen.

She waited, half expecting the woman to reappear, but now the garden was entirely empty.

CHAPTER NINE

THE FOLLOWING MORNING, AS she made her way into the house through the back door, Fanny heard a sound that was shocking and entirely unexpected.

Laughter.

Stopping in her tracks, she listened as muffled voices rang out through the house. Richard and Rebecca were in the study, or perhaps the library, and they seemed to be getting along rather well. After a few seconds Fanny made her way to the table by the window and set her basket down, and then she lingered again as the laughter continued. A moment later, as footsteps suddenly hurried across the hallway, she turned and began to arrange the items from the basket, acting as if she had not even noticed the strange sound.

"Someone's having a good morning," Oliver said as he wandered into the kitchen, with his heavy work boots thudding hard against the bare wooden floor. "Sounds like they're getting on just fine."

"Indeed," Fanny said through pursed lips.

"I was meaning to speak to Mr. Hadlow about something," Oliver continued, stopping and looking out the window, "but perhaps I'll wait until he's better able to focus."

He paused, before turning to his wife.

"He needs to know what happened, Fanny."

"What are you talking about?" she asked, attempting to focus on the greens in the basket.

"You know exactly what I'm -"

"No, I do not," she said firmly, cutting him off as he took her paring knife and began to strip some of the leaves. "It *sounds* as if you're about to suggest something utterly stupid, but that cannot be the case. After all, we have discussed this matter at great length and I know full well that you would not wish to reopen that discussion." She turned and glared at him, as if she hoped to use the sheer force of her stare to batter him into submission. "I'm not married to a fool, Oliver... am I?"

"I just think we should tell him."

"For what purpose?"

He opened his mouth to reply, but instead he found himself searching for the right words.

"To salve your conscience?" she asked,

lowering her voice a little as laughter continued to ring out from the front of the house. "That is what prayer is for, Oliver. The Lord sees everything. He saw what happened that day, and what we did. He understands that we made the right choice." She paused, watching him intently as if she was still worried that he might be about to contradict her. "And the matter is settled," she added. "In the eyes of God, and in our eyes as well, and most certainly in Mr. Hadlow's eyes. Let us not cause disruption where none is necessary."

Again Oliver seemed poised to reply. After a few seconds, however, he turned and looked toward the open door.

"They sound happy," he pointed out finally. "I suppose it would be wrong to do anything that might risk such a miracle."

"There's no miracle," she muttered. "It's just people getting on with their lives, in the best way that they can. Speaking of which, do you not have any tasks at all that require your attention? I was under the impression that you had a river to dredge, and a tree to fix, and all manner of other jobs around the house."

"Aye, that I do," he admitted, and then he hesitated yet again. "Fanny, just one thing," he added. "Do you think it was quick? What I mean is, do you think -"

"Oliver!" she snapped, suddenly stepping

toward him and holding the paring knife up as if she meant to slide its blade into his face. "Will you shut up?"

Shocked by his wife's anger, Oliver simply stared at her until – after a few seconds – she lowered the knife. He watched as she rubbed one side of her face, and then as she returned to her work with the greens in the basket.

"That's quite enough of that," she said, clearly shaken by her own outburst. "We agreed to never speak of such things, so let us never speak of them. And remember, Mr. Hadlow will not be happy if he doesn't see you getting on with your labors."

***

"I assure you, it's all true," Richard said in the study, with a smile on his face as he leaned against the wall and watched Rebecca looking through one of his books. "One would scarcely be able to make up such a tale."

"There is much humor in the world," she replied, glancing up at him with a grin. "And you do tell a tale so very well."

"Can you read that book?" he asked. "Obviously you can read it, I know that, but can you comprehend what it is saying?"

"I believe so."

"Then you are a marvel," he told her. "I am

not one of those men who believe women to have vastly inferior minds, but still I would have thought that such lofty ideas are above you."

She looked down and turned to another page in the book, and she took a moment to read the text.

"I think I understand," she said cautiously. "It is a treatise on religion, is it not?"

"It is."

"I confess," she continued, "I do not understand why men fight over -"

Stopping suddenly, she looked at him with fear in her eyes.

"Go on," he said. "You must have full confidence here in our home to say whatever it is that is on your mind."

"I only mean," she replied, "that there has been such violence in the land of late. Men fighting their neighbors, killing people, causing great devastation. We are only forty or so years removed from a schism that almost divided England in two, and then recently the very same thing nearly happened again, all because one group of people believe that another group should not worship in a certain way." She paused, before closing the book. "I simply do not understand the keenness of some men to act like that. Is not God... always God?"

"That is an interesting way to put it," he told her.

"Do you think the old king will ever come

back?"

"No," Richard replied. "I believe he will die in France."

"And the present king and queen," she added cautiously, "will continue to reign?" She glanced around, as if she was still worried about being overheard. "My father believes that there might yet be threats to them, especially if matters in Ireland do not go a certain way. In truth, my father obsesses over such things and tries to determine the future with certainty."

"No man can do that," Richard told her. "What I *can* tell you is that my own father was one of the men you described a moment ago. He believed that he had the right to kill other men in the name of his version of God."

"And he died for that?"

Richard nodded.

"And that," she continued cautiously, "is why you wished to make this clean break, is it not?"

He paused, and then he nodded again.

"And perhaps why, despite your wealth," she added, "you had to marry the daughter of a rather poor London draper, instead of someone more worthy of your stature."

"I would not have married anyone else," he told her.

"But you did."

"That is different," he said with a sigh.

"Rebecca, I do not wish to get into such matters now, but let me assure you that I am very happy with how things are now. I truly believe that we have a bright future together, and that we can build our own lives without having to constantly refer to our pasts. This house is a symbol of that. One year ago, this was a mere clearing in the forest."

"I still cannot believe that such a beautiful house could have been built so quickly," she told him.

"When one has the means and the determination," he replied, "one can achieve almost anything that one desires. And this house is what I desired, so I had it built. And then I desired to have a wife here, and I found you. There is really no need to go into the past and rake it all up, because one cannot change the past, no matter how hard one tries. One can only change the future, so that – I believe – is where one's efforts should be directed. If I am wrong, I am wrong." Spotting movement, he looked out the window and saw Oliver walking across the garden. "And now, if you will excuse me," he added, "I must speak to Oliver about some matters. Please, sit here for as long as you wish and look at the books. You must not feel pressured into doing anything that you do not want to do."

AMY CROSS

CHAPTER TEN

"THIS TREE IS DYING," Oliver said as he stood at the far end of the garden, looking up at the branches of the old oak tree. "You can see it there, and there."

He pointed to one particular long, gnarly branch.

"And there especially," he added.

"Can anything be done?" Richard asked. "I confess, I have a fondness for this thing. I know it's just a tree, but it has been here for a long time and I should not like it to fall on my watch."

"I can try cutting off the damaged sections," Oliver told him. "My own father told me that sometimes it works to do that, although there are no guarantees."

"Do that, then," Richard replied. "I trust

you, Oliver, and I know that if the tree can be saved, you'll save it."

"Would you like me to get on with that work this morning, before I start in the river?"

"I would not dare to tell you how to organize your time," Richard continued, before patting him on the shoulder. "I have been thinking that I might take Rebecca out to show her some of the forest. The area surrounding this house is absolutely beautiful, and it's only fitting that she should see the local wildlife. If you have no need of my assistance, I shall leave you to work in peace."

"That sounds fitting, Sir," Oliver told him. "Thank you."

He paused.

"But there is one other matter, Sir," he added, glancing at the house and seeing that Fanny was nowhere to be seen. "I shouldn't mention it," he continued, lowering his voice, "but something has been on my mind. My wife believes that it should be forgotten, yet I think that a man in your position would like to know."

"What are you talking about?" Richard asked.

"It's about the previous Mrs. Hadlow. Your first wife. If you don't mind -"

"I really don't wish to know," Richard said firmly, cutting him off before he could get another word out. "I'm sorry, Oliver, but I don't think that this is the appropriate time to be bringing that matter up. I am extremely grateful to you and your wife for your assistance during that difficult time, but it is in the past and I think it should be left there. What happened to Catherine was horribly unfortunate, but she is gone and Rebecca is here and I would not change that for the world. Do you understand?"

Oliver hesitated, before nodding slightly.

"Then we are in agreement," Richard told him with a smile. "Let us try to stay that way."

As Richard walked away, Oliver put his hands on his hips and stared up at the branches of the oak tree. He knew he should get to the river and start pulling out the weeds, but in truth he was already trying to work out exactly which of the tree's branches should be removed first, and after a moment he told himself that this particular job only needed to take a few hours

***

"Mrs. Baxter, might I ask you something?"

Looking up from the rabbit she'd been busy skinning, Fanny saw that Rebecca was standing in the kitchen doorway, watching her with a strange expression of apprehension.

"Do you want to learn how to skin one of these things?" Fanny asked.

"It's not about that," Rebecca said, before making her way over. She seemed nervous and more than a little agitated. "It's about last night."

"Your first night in Hadlow House?"

Rebecca moved even closer and leaned across the table.

"How do I know," she whispered, "whether the marriage was... consummated?"

Fanny raised a skeptical eyebrow.

"We slept in the same bed," Rebecca continued. "Does that mean..."

She paused, before placing both hands on her flat belly.

"You were raised by your father, were you not?" Fanny said cautiously. "Did you have any female supervision at all?"

Rebecca shook her head.

"Did Mr. Hadlow position himself on top of you in the bed?" Fanny asked.

"On top of me?" Rebecca furrowed her brow. "In no way, shape or form. Why?"

"Certain things would have to happen before you might be with child," Fanny told her. "Merely sleeping in the same bed would not bring such a condition about."

"Are you sure?"

"Quite sure."

"Do you have children of your own?" Rebecca asked.

"Mr. Baxter and I were never blessed in that way," Fanny told her.

"I'm sorry to have come to you with such questions," Rebecca continued. "It's just that I want to be a good wife to Richard, really I do, now that I have realized that this is my role. In truth, I do not know what I expected to happen last night, but I got the impression that Richard wanted to do something yet he was not quite able to... get started."

"Is that so?" Fanny replied, and now she seemed faintly amused.

"He put a hand on my leg," Rebecca explained. "Just one hand, just above the knee. But his hand was shaking, almost trembling with fear. There was a moment of intensity that seemed ready to break into some kind of act, and then he withdrew his hand and told me that he hoped I would sleep well." She sighed. "I do not know what I am supposed to do in such situation," she added. "All I know is that I must love my husband."

"Love?" Fanny said, and now her sense of amusement seemed to be growing.

"Isn't that important between a husband and a wife?" Rebecca asked.

"Let me tell you something about love," Fanny replied, setting the paring knife down. "Have you ever seen two dogs rutting? Or any animals, really?"

"I do not think so."

"If you had," Fanny continued, "you would know that love is a bitter, harsh and brutal exchange. It is violent and painful, and there is absolutely no pleasure to be take from it at all."

"There isn't?" Rebecca said, and now she seemed disappointed. "But I thought -"

"Love is a technical matter between a man and a woman," Fanny said firmly, "and it requires a certain degree of force on the man's part to make it work. The woman, in turn, must arrange herself in a position that aids the man in his mission." She paused, watching the confusion in Rebecca's eyes. "If the act gives either participant pleasure," she continued, "then it is being done wrong. Pain in the act of love is not only natural, it is necessary. The more pain you feel, the better."

"Oh."

"You can even assist yourself in this matter," Fanny told her. "A small blade, secreted about your person, can be used to bring even more pain. Mind, you should only use it on yourself." She picked up the paring knife and wiped most of the rabbit's blood away, before handing it to Rebecca. "Something like this would be perfect," she added. "Hold it hidden in your hand, perhaps, and squeeze tight until the blade cuts your palm. You must feel the pain and embrace it. You must have tears in your eyes." She tilted her head slightly, and now her own eyes were wide with pleasure. "It must hurt if it is being done correctly."

"Oh," Rebecca said again, looking down at the knife in her left hand. "I knew none of this."

"Well, that is no surprise," Fanny said, "if indeed you were raised solely by your father. It's understandable that you would know nothing of love." She leaned a little closer, until her face was just inches from Rebecca's own. "If you want to truly prove your love to Richard," she added, "you should try to remain completely unresponsive while you feel the pain. Don't scream. Instead, take all of that pain inside your body. I should not tell you this, but one thing I find useful is to use the knife's blade and make cuts inside yourself." She reached down and touched the front of Rebecca's dress. "You know what I mean. Cut yourself regularly and deeply, so that when your husband loves you there is much blood. And if you find any part of your body that rises and swells to the temptation of pleasure, you must cut that out entirely, do you understand?"

"Y... yes..." Rebecca stammered. "I think so."

"Go and do it now," Fanny sneered. "Go and _"

"Ladies!"

Startled, they both turned to see that Richard was making his way through. Fanny immediately stepped away from Rebecca, who in turn set the knife down on the counter.

"Rebecca," Richard said, clearly unaware of any tension in the room as he took her by the hand, "I was thinking that I might take you for a short walk, to show you some of the local area. The wildflowers in particular are quite beautiful at this time of year."

"That would be lovely," Rebecca replied, allowing him to lead her out of the kitchen. "Thank you, Mrs. Baxter," she added, glancing over her shoulder. "You have been most helpful."

Fanny smiled and waited for them to leave the room, and then she turned and took the knife again before picking up the skinned rabbit. She admired the sinewy muscles and tendons for a moment, before cutting away part of the muscle and slipping the raw meat into her mouth.

"My dear," she whispered with a smile, "you are most welcome."

CHAPTER ELEVEN

"DAMN IT!" OLIVER HISSED, straddling one of the oak tree's branches while he tried to cut the next branch along. "This thing is too rusty!"

Taking a look at the saw, he realized that its teeth was far too ragged and damaged. He'd been up in the tree for a few minutes now, cutting like crazy but making little progress. He had several other saws down on the ground, and he knew that most of them would be more effective, but climbing into the tree had taken quite some time and he wanted to avoid having to go all the way back down.

"Infernal thing," he sighed, before running a fingertip against the saw's rusty teeth. He felt the sharpness, although he was careful to avoid cutting himself. "What are we going to do with you? You're no good for anything and -"

Hearing voices, he turned and looked toward the house, just in time to spot Richard and Rebecca making their way past the edge of the garden and out toward the forest.

"Sir?" Oliver called out, waving at them in the hope that his employer might be able to pass one of the better saws up for him to use. "Sir, might I have some assistance?"

He waited, but after a moment he sighed again as he realized that he hadn't been heard. Sure enough, Richard and Rebecca walked off between the trees, laughing as they talked to each other, and Oliver realized that this window of opportunity had closed.

"Sir!" he called out anyway, just in case he might get lucky. "I'm sorry to disturb you, Sir, but is there any chance that you might be able to come over and..."

His voice trailed off as he realized that he was too late.

"Damn and bother," he complained under his breath. "Then again..."

Then again, he hated the idea of admitting to any kind of weakness. After all, who would want to employ a groundskeeper and general handyman who lacked sufficient strength to complete even the most basic of tasks.

Looking at the saws on the ground again, he considered climbing back down, but recent pains in his lower back made him reconsider. At the same time, he also knew that the job of cutting off the branch would take much longer if he didn't have the right equipment, and he felt that he was rather trapped between two options. A moment later he spotted movement again; he looked toward the house, and this time he saw that Fanny had made her way around to the side and was pouring some water out onto the ground.

"Fanny!" Oliver shouted, waving at her.

"What?" she called back to him.

"Can you give me a hand with something?" he asked.

"Not now," she replied. "I'm busy."

"It's just a small thing!" he told her. "Fanny, please, can you pass one of the other saws up to me? It was hard enough climbing up here, I certainly don't want to do it all over again."

"You should have thought about that earlier, then," she told him. "You're not the only one who has things to do, Oliver. Do you have any idea how busy I am at the moment?"

With that, she carried the bucket back into the house, leaving Oliver to let out a heavy sigh as he realized that his last chance of help had faded. He sat for a few seconds, thinking once again about his next step, and finally he supposed that his best bet was simply to work with the saw in his hands and get the branch cut as quickly as possible. After taking a moment to prepare himself, he shuffled along the first branch and reached out, placing the saw's teeth against the next branch. He paused again, fully aware of the physical labor to come, and then he began to saw the branch away.

"Come on," he muttered under his breath as he felt the rusty teeth struggling to cut through even this rotten wood. "Just because you're old, that doesn't mean you're excused for working. If the world worked like that, I'd be sitting around right now living an easy life, instead of working my hide off for Mr. Hadlow."

For the next couple of minutes he continued to saw, but he had to admit that the effort was starting to make him feel more tired than he'd expected. He was barely a quarter of the way through the branch, but already he had to stop for a moment and take a breather. Reaching up, he wiped sweat from his hot brow, and already he could feel aches and pains rippling all over his tired frame, and he told himself that he could still get the job done.

And then, hearing a scratching sound nearby, he turned and looked down toward the ground.

He waited, and already his heart was racing. The scratching sound seemed to be coming from somewhere nearby, and it was the same sound he'd heard on a number of occasions already. He knew that Fanny sometimes heard the same sound, but his wife always refused to discuss the matter, insisting that some natural phenomenon must be the cause; for Oliver, however, this persistent scratching sound seemed to be filled with a level of urgency that he felt could only mean one thing. He waited, listening as the sound continued, and finally one name slipped from his lips.

"Catherine?"

A shudder passed through his chest, and after a moment he realized that the entire garden had fallen silent. Until that moment he hadn't paid any attention to the rustle of trees and the occasional tweet of birds; he only noticed them now that they were gone, but as he turned and looked around he heard not even the slightest hint of movement anywhere. If he hadn't known better, he could have believed in that moment that he was the only living creature left in the whole world.

Except for the scratching sound coming from somewhere on the ground.

"Fanny?" he called out, trying to stay calm. "Fanny, can you hear me?"

He waited, feeling sure that his wife would emerge from the house soon. After all, she should certainly be able to hear him, even if she believed herself to be too busy.

"Fanny!" he shouted, raising his voice. "Fanny, where are you? For the love of all that's holy, can't you just come out here for a moment?"

As the forest remained silent, Oliver looked back down at the ground. The scratching sound seemed to have become more frantic now, and he couldn't help but imagine bony dead fingertips scraping furiously against wood. He told himself once again that he was letting his imagination run wild, and finally he realized that there was really only one sensible option.

"Fanny?" he yelled one more time, but he reasoned that he was being ignored.

Determined to get the job done and climb down from the tree, he started sawing once again, working hard and fast as he tried to cut through the branch. He was sweating more heavily than ever, with drips falling now from his face, and he noticed after a few more seconds that he was feeling a little faint. He wanted to stop and take a short rest, but he worried that he might not get going again; he began to saw even harder, while trying to ignore the sense of panic that was filling his body. The saw's teeth was screeching and grinding loudly against the branch, yet somehow even this noise was not loud enough to entirely drown out the sound of scratching.

So he worked harder.

And faster.

Pushing through the pain, he began to curse under his breath as he tried to cut through the branch. The saw's rusty teeth were catching with each stroke, ripping through the wood with force but making precious little progress. Oliver adjusted his angle of attack a little, trying over and over to find different ways he might be able to force the saw deeper, but more and more sweat was running down his face now and he felt a sharp pain bursting through his body. He almost slipped from the branch, and he had to take a moment to steady himself before resuming his work, sawing so fast now that he felt there was nothing more he could possibly do, until finally he blinked and in that moment he suddenly saw what had actually happened.

As the scratching sound continued nearby, sounding so loud now that it almost seemed to be *inside* his ears, his eyes opened wide with shock.

Somehow he'd not been sawing through the branch at all. Instead, he'd cut straight through his own left arm, sawing it off just below the elbow and sending blood gushing from the stump and splattering onto the ground below.

CHAPTER TWELVE

"I'VE BANDAGED IT TIGHT," Fanny said a couple of hours later as she stood with Richard in the study, "and that should do for now, but he'll have to be seen by someone who knows better."

"It's too late in the day now to take him anywhere," Richard told her. "Will he last until morning?"

"I believe so," she replied, although she sounded a little doubtful. "He lost so much blood. I don't know what he can have been thinking, he was half delirious when I found him. It's one thing for a man to accidentally cut himself, but he looks to have taken the saw to his own arm and removed it entirely. Why would he do such at thing?"

"I'm sure he'll be able to explain once he's up on his feet again."

"He'll be no use to you now, Sir," she added, with a hint of tears in her eyes. "If I might be so bold, would you mind if we stay for at least a few weeks before we have to leave?"

"Leave?"

"Your employment, Sir."

"There's no question of that," he told her. "Fanny, you and Oliver served my father with exemplary attention to detail, as you have served me since his death. The idea of throwing the pair of you out is simply unconscionable."

"But his arm -"

"We will manage," he said firmly, placing a hand on her shoulder. "You and Oliver are like family to me, Fanny, and I could no sooner turn you out into the cold as I could leave this house myself. You are free to leave, there is no doubt about that, but I would like you to stay. Please, let me help you in your hour of need."

"You are too kind, Sir," she replied, before reaching up to wipe a tear from her cheek.

"Don't worry about your duties for now," he continued. "Rebecca and I are not infants, we can look after ourselves while you tend to your husband. I want you to prioritize his care and make sure that he has every chance to recover as much of his strength as possible. There will be time to think about the future, but right now your husband needs you."

"You are too kind," she told him. "Sometimes, Mr. Hadlow, you remind me of..."

She hesitated, as if she suddenly worried that she might say too much.

"Well, of your father," she added. "In some ways. In your character, at least."

"That is kind of you to say," he replied, clearly bristling slightly as he took a step back. "Go to Oliver and tend to his needs. Please. Rebecca and I will be just fine."

***

"We're not to be thrown out onto the streets, at least," Fanny said once she'd returned to the cramped room she and Oliver shared near the back of the house. "Thank heavens for small mercies, but it's no thanks to you."

Resting on the bed, with his left arm heavily bandaged, Oliver winced as he continued to stare up at the ceiling.

"You've always been a simple man," Fanny continued, taking a moment to arrange some clothes that had been left on the table by the window, "but this is something entirely new. How does any sane man, any man with even an ounce of sense, cut his own arm off?" She glanced at him, her expression filled with withering disapproval. "I cannot fathom what must have been going through your head, but you are evidently a far more foolish man than even I believed. And that, I must tell you, is some revelation."

"It was her," he whispered.

"I beg your pardon?"

"It was her," he said again, still not looking at his wife. "As the Lord is my witness, Fanny, it was Catherine Hadlow."

"What are you talking about?" she snapped, before hurrying back across the room and pushing the door gently shut so that they could not possibly be overheard. She hesitated, and then she turned to look back at Oliver. "Have you taken leave of your senses?"

"I heard her," he replied. "Scratching."

"You -"

"I heard her, Fanny!" he said firmly, finally turning to her. Sweat was glistening on his brow. "I heard her fingers scratching on the wood."

"Catherine Hadlow is dead," she told him. "We buried her ourselves."

"I know."

She opened her mouth to reply, but for a moment she held back. Finally, stepping around the bed, she stopped to look directly down into her husband's eyes.

"She's back, Fanny," he continued, his voice tense with fear. "I don't know how, and I don't want to find out how, but she's come back to make us pay for what we did to her."

"We buried her," she replied. "That is all."

"It's not all, and you know it."

"You must have a fever," she said, perching on the side of the bed and reaching over, placing the back of one hand against his forehead. "Yes, it's true, I feel it. Your temperature is high. There's a chance that your wound is infected, though I cleaned it as best as I could manage."

"She is returning."

"The dead do not return, Oliver."

"I heard her scratching!" he hissed. "I know what I -"

Suddenly he let out a pained gasp as Fanny pressed her right hand against the bloodied bandages on his stump. At the same time she placed her other hand over his mouth, stifling any cries he might let out, and then she dug two fingers between the bandaged and into the pulp around the exposed bone of his forearm. Oliver's entire body shuddered as he tried to pull away, but he was weak now and his wife's strength kept him in place as she wriggled her fingers inside his body. As Oliver struggled, the wooden bed creaked and Fanny's fingers made a squelching sound in the bloodied wound.

"I wouldn't talk of such things, if I were you," she told him, as she pushed her fingers deeper, sliding them between bone and meat. "You're letting your emotions get the better of you,

Oliver, and that is not a good thing."

He tried again to cry out, but Fanny merely tightened her hand's grip over his mouth. Meanwhile she twisted her fingers, letting her fingernails slice the inside of his wound.

"I need you to be calm," she continued. "This is love I am showing for you right now, Oliver. A wife has many jobs, and one of those jobs is to keep her husband on the right track whenever he shows weakness." She began wriggling her fingers inside the wound, as fresh blood poured out onto the bed's sheets. "Can I trust you or do I have to go to even greater lengths in my attempt to teach you this lesson?"

"Stop!" he managed to hiss as he turned his head, but she quickly covered his mouth again.

"I never imagined that I would be married to a fool," she said, leaning over him as her fingers pressed harder against the bone of his arm. "I would rather not have that be the case, Oliver. Catherine Hadlow is dead, and her body is buried out by the tree, and that means she is gone. Do you understand? She is dead and gone, and no amount of feverish rambling will bring her back. Can you get that into your head?"

She hesitated, before pulling her hand away from his mouth.

"Stop!" he sobbed.

"Tell me you are no fool!"

"I'm no fool!"

She pulled her fingers out of his wound and rearranged the bandages. Already a lot of blood had soaked into the bed, with some having dribbled down onto the bare wooden floorboards.

"Let there be no more talk of dead women returning from the grave," Fanny said a little breathlessly. "I've warned you now, Oliver, and I expect that to be the end of the matter. Indeed, you should make sure that you have a very good reason if you ever utter the name Catherine Hadlow again. Her body is buried and her memory should be as well." She paused, watching her husband's face as if she was searching for even the slightest hint that he might rebel against her instructions. "And now," she added, heading to the door, "I must go and see what needs doing downstairs. My life is going to be even harder now that I am married to a cripple."

She cast one last disdainful glance at him, before opening the door and stepping out of the room.

Left alone on the bed, Oliver began to slowly look around the room. All he saw were gloomy, empty spaces, but he couldn't help worrying that at any moment he might spot the ghostly form of Catherine Hadlow.

AMY CROSS

CHAPTER THIRTEEN

"WHAT?"

Opening her eyes, Rebecca found herself staring up at the bedroom's dark ceiling. She blinked, and for a few seconds she believed herself to be back in London, in her father's house; when she blinked again she remembered the journey to Kent, and a moment later she turned and saw her husband sleeping soundly on the bed's other side.

Husband.

Such a strange word, and one that still felt very alien to her every sensibility. Still, she quickly reminded herself that she could have ended up married to a much worse man, and that so far Richard Hadlow seemed kind and caring. Perhaps in her youth Rebecca had entertained some notion of falling in love and marrying for that reason, but she knew such matches were exceedingly rare; instead she had been promised by her father to this Hadlow man, whose past seemed a little troublesome, but overall she had landed very much on her feet. Indeed, she had resolved now to work hard and try to become the best possible wife.

Suddenly hearing a creaking sound, she turned and looked toward the door. She heard the sound again, and now she knew that someone was out on the landing. Thinking back to the hand she'd felt on her shoulder on her first day at the house, she found herself wondering whether there might be some unseen figure lurking in the shadows, but a moment later she heard a gruff cough and all her fears faded.

Getting to her feet, she checked that Richard was still asleep and then she tip-toed across the room. As soon as she opened the door, she saw that poor Oliver was very slowly making his way down the stairs.

"Mr. Baxter," she whispered, before stepping onto the landing and pulling the bedroom door shut. "Is there something you require? If your wife is asleep, I would be more than happy to assist you in any way necessary."

Oliver looked up at her, and Rebecca was immediately taken aback by the expression of fear in the old man's eyes. He kept his gaze fixed upon her with unusual intensity for several more seconds, before muttering something under his breath and looking down toward the hallway. After a moment he started walking again, while still clutching his damaged left arm just above the elbow.

"Are you quite alright?" Rebecca asked, stepping over to the top of the stairs and watching as he continued his slow and painful progression down. "Mr. Baxter?"

Ignoring her, he reached the bottom of the stairs and shuffled out of sight, leaving Rebecca wondering exactly how she should respond. She barely knew Oliver, of course, and she certainly had no great understanding of his character; at the same time, she felt that no man should be up and about in the middle of the night, especially having recently suffered such a grievous injury.

A moment later she heard a brief but heavy clicking sound coming from somewhere toward the rear of the house. Recognizing this as the sound of the back door opening, she turned and hurried to one of the windows, and she looked out across the moonlit garden just in time to spot Oliver slowly walking away from the house.

"Where are you going?" she whispered.

***

"Mr. Baxter?"

Despite the cold temperature, Rebecca had

wrapped herself in a gown and made her way out of the back door, and now she'd stopped at the far end of the garden. Ahead, Oliver was standing with his back to her, staring down at a spot of dirt near the old oak tree.

"Mr. Baxter?" she said again. "Can I help you with anything?"

She waited again, but she was starting to wonder whether the old man had lost his hearing. Either that, or could he possibly be walking around in his sleep? Rebecca had heard about such things from her father, although she had no idea how she should approach somebody in such a position. A moment later, just as she was starting to wonder whether she should go closer, she saw Oliver slowly getting down onto his knees, and then she watched as he leaned forward and used his one remaining hand to start pulling away some of the weeds.

Stepping forward, Rebecca made her way around Oliver and looked down to see that he appeared to be trying to clear an area on the ground. At first she thought that he could be trying to bury something, but after a few more seconds she spotted what appeared to be an old crucifix that had been partially buried in the dirt. Confused, she crouched down and watched as Oliver ripped away more plants, and then she saw him trying to pull the crucifix up from the ground.

"What is that for?" she asked.

Oliver murmured something, but she was unable to make out his words.

"Can I help you?" she continued.

He continued to pull on the crucifix, but – with only one hand – he was clearly struggling.

"Here," she said, reaching over and carefully taking hold of the crucifix's lower end, then using her fingertips to tease it from the dried mud.

Sure enough, together they were soon able to lift the crucifix up. Rebecca let go, leaving Oliver to hold the crucifix up in the moonlight; an expression of shock filled the old man's eyes now, as if he couldn't quite believe what he was seeing, and his mouth hung open as a few faint grunts emerged from the back of his throat.

"It was Fanny's idea to put this here," he said finally. "I forget her reasoning now, but I think she said something at the time about wanting to show respect. But it can't have been about respect, can it? Not if she then encouraged weeds to grow over the grave."

"Grave?" Rebecca said cautiously. "Is somebody buried here?"

"Mr. Hadlow insisted," Oliver continued, still admiring the crucifix with a growing sense of awe, "so Fanny said that we had to do it in a certain way. Mr. Hadlow left the details to her, you see, and she went to great trouble to procure this cross, and then she insisted that it had to be placed securely on the grave. I suppose I believed her when she said that it was a mark of respect, but now I find myself wondering if there might have been some other motive. Could this cross have somehow been an attempt to..."

He paused, before looking down at the dirt.

"I heard about something similar once," he explained. "A man in the north, fearful of a haunting, was said to have placed such a cross on the door of his bedroom, to ward the spirits away. If that worked for him, then would perhaps it work here too? Just in a different way, to keep..."

He hesitated as a shudder passed through his bones.

"To stop something rising up," he whispered. "I've heard her scratching, but that doesn't make sense since she was buried not in a coffin but in a simple sack. So she couldn't be scratching on the inside of a coffin lid, even if that's what it sounded like, because there's no lid down there. Still, I can't help thinking that it's her way of letting us know she wants to come up. Many's the time of late that I've thought she might be nearby, that she's strained to reach out of her grave." He paused, before setting the cross down near the base of the tree. "There," he added. "I've done it now, if indeed there's anything to be done at all. If she wants to come up properly, she can do so. I only hope that she can find it in her heart to show us a little mercy."

He turned to Rebecca.

"A man can't hide from such things forever," he told her. "The dead will always find a way. There's no point trying to stop them. Besides, if she sees that I'm the one who helped free her spirit, she might be kinder to me. Don't you think so?"

"I truly know not what to say," she replied, shivering a little in the cold air. "I confess that I am but a simple girl from London. You speak of strange things, Mr. Baxter, of which I know almost nothing."

"Then keep it that way," he said, "and go inside and return to your bed. I shall be back inside presently, I assure you. And in the morning, please say nothing of this moment to anyone else. Especially not to my wife. I'm probably wrong, I'm probably a fool but..."

He hesitated, and then he turned and looked down once again at the dirt.

"But it's better to be safe," he added darkly, "and to beg for forgiveness from those that might have been wronged."

AMY CROSS

CHAPTER FOURTEEN

"I THOUGHT THAT PERHAPS today I might take you into the village," Richard said the following morning, as he set his dirty plate down on the table and turned to Rebecca. "You would enjoy that, would you not?"

Having barely heard a word her husband had said during breakfast, Rebecca continued to stare at the window for a moment before turning to him. Her mind was racing now, and she was dimly aware that he had just asked her opinion about something, and she felt awful for having not paid any attention.

"You seem a little out of sorts," he continued. "Perhaps a journey to the village would be too much and -"

"No!" she blurted out quickly, relieved to

understand exactly what he had asked. "I would like that very much."

"Are you alright?"

"I confess that I did not sleep last night as well as I might have done," she told him, before hearing a faint pattering sound nearby.

Turning, she saw that rain was falling outside and tapping lightly at the window.

"And I have a headache," she added, realizing that this was true enough. Reaching up, she touched the back of her head, slipping her fingertips into her hair. "Just a small one," she continued, "but it is enough to serve as a distraction and I am afraid that I do not quite feel like myself."

"Then a trip to the village is out of the question," Richard told her, "especially since the weather seems to have turned." He peered past her, before heading to one of the other windows and looking up just as a dribble of water began to run from the inside of the frame. "I thought Oliver had fixed all these small holes," he muttered, clearly annoyed as he wiped the dribble away, only for another bead to swiftly form. "I shall have to get him to check again once he's well."

At that moment, Fanny made her way into the kitchen and placed a large basket on the counter, while muttering away to herself under her breath.

"I shouldn't think that Oliver will be up for any work soon, however," Richard continued. "That being the case, I suppose I shall take on some of his duties around the house for a while. Why, I do not see why it should be beyond me to fix a hole in the wall, or even to dredge that foul river out there. Fanny, do you think there is any reason why your husband would begrudge me the opportunity to get my hands dirty in such a manner?"

"I'm sorry?"

Fanny turned to him, then to Rebecca, and then to her master again.

"You too," Richard murmured, rolling his eyes. "Evidently I am not to be listened to very much today, but I suppose that as a married man I should get used to that. Fanny, I was just telling my wife that I thought I might take her to Cobblefield this morning, but now I think I shall wait for a day with better weather. Do you think you might find some way to keep her busy while I do some work outside?"

"I'm sure I can come up with something," Fanny said, although she didn't sound too enthusiastic. "Oliver's resting, so I have twice as much work as usual to get done and I could use a little help." She turned to Rebecca. "Would you like me to show you how to make one of Mr. Hadlow's favorite meals?"

"Is this the rabbit stew?" Richard asked.

"It most certainly is," Fanny continued. "All young brides must swiftly learn to keep their husbands well fed, and Rebecca is no exception. I do not mean to overstep my position, Mr. Hadlow, but I believe that one of my responsibilities now should be to ease your lovely wife into certain new ways and habits." She turned to Rebecca. "I hope you will not consider me immodest, Mrs. Hadlow, if I say that I believe I have mastered the art of feeding a man properly."

"Immodest?" Rebecca replied with a smile. "Mrs. Baxter, on the contrary, I think you are a woman of very many talents and I would be so grateful to learn at your feet. Should you have the time and patience to teach me, of course."

"We shall see what can be made of you," Fanny told her, before turning again to Richard. "You can leave your wife in my capable hands, Sir. In fact, I think I shall rather enjoy this challenge."

***

A few hours later, Rebecca finished dicing the last of the rabbit meat and stopped for a moment to admire her work. Her right arm was aching a little from all the repetitive work, but she felt a rush of pride as she realized that she'd followed Fanny's instructions with perfect precision.

"Excellent work," Fanny said, making her way over to inspect the results. She even allowed herself a faint, unaccustomed smile. "You have potential."

"I just want to make Richard happy."

"There's still a lot more to do," Fanny pointed out. "Now, can you go through into the storeroom beyond the pantry and find me a pot that will be suitable for the stew. Make sure it's one with a heavy base and a wide open top. Remember that this stew is going to cook for a number of hours, so there will be a reduction in the amount of water."

"Of course," Rebecca said, keen to help as she turned and hurried toward the door in the corner. "I'll be quick."

"There's no need to rush around," Fanny told her. "Indeed, rushing is one of the surest ways of making a mistake."

"Absolutely."

Rebecca slowed her pace as she headed into the pantry, and she tried to take this latest lesson onboard as she made her way into the storage room at the far end. Spotting various pots and pans, she tried to work out which might be correct, and she couldn't help but feel that this was another small test. She desperately wanted to prove her own worth to Mrs. Baxter, so she took a couple of minutes to examine the various pots before picking it up and – finding it to be rather heavy – turning to head back through.

And then, stopping suddenly, she saw a human hand poking out from under a fabric sheet on one of the shelves. Shocked, she froze for a few seconds before setting the pot back down and heading over to inspect the hand more closely. Lifting the fabric a little, she saw to her horror that someone – Mrs. Baxter, she assumed – had evidently seen fit to keep Oliver's severed arm in this manner.

Wincing slightly, Rebecca told herself that she shouldn't interfere, but after a few seconds she found herself staring at the bloodied stump at the end of the forearm. She hesitated, before stepping a little closer so that she could see the discolored meat packed around the ragged and broken bone. Peering at the damage, she was just about able to make out what she could only assume must be the marrow within the bone. She felt utter shock at the sight of such a thing, but she also began to realize that for some reason she was unable to turn away.

Her lips parted slightly.

She looked over her shoulder, to make sure that there was no chance of Fanny appearing, and then she leaned closer to the severed arm and looked more carefully at the meat. She'd briefly glimpsed a lot of blood when Oliver had first lost his arm, but now the man's arm appeared to have changed color slightly, and she reasoned that it was most likely beginning the slow process of rotting. That idea horrified her, yet she also found herself strangely fascinated, until slowly she reached out and touched the meaty stump. As soon as she felt the cold flesh, she felt a shiver of anticipation run through her body, and she began to realize that she was filling with the most unnatural urge.

After looking over her shoulder again, she began to pull on the torn meat, finally ripping a small chunk away. Holding it up, she realized that it looked not entirely unlike the rabbit meat in the kitchen; she turned this lump of Oliver's arm around, admiring the way that it glistened in the low light, and then – before she could stop herself – she slipped this lump between her lips and bit down on it. As soon as she tasted the old blood, she felt a shiver of pleasure, and she quickly pulled off another lump and set this too into her mouth. She chewed for a few seconds, and then she dared herself to do the unthinkable.

She swallowed.

Although her mind knew that what she was doing was wrong, Rebecca was unable to stop herself; she pulled off another piece of meat, a strip this time, then another, and soon she was chewing several of these pieces at once. The idea of leaving such perfect meat alone seemed impossible, and she began to wonder whether she might be able to chew the arm clean until nothing was left expect bone. Deep down she understood that this was a most unnatural practice, that no person should consume part of another, yet as the pain in the back of her head began to throb she knew that she could not possibly resist such temptation.

Finally she picked up the arm and began to chew directly from the flesh, even letting her teeth scrape against the bone.

"Rebecca?" Fanny called out suddenly. "Do you need help?"

"No!" she gasped, setting the arm down and recovering it, then taking a moment to wipe her mouth before swallowing the last of the meat and grabbing the pot. "I'm coming!"

As she hurried back through to the kitchen, she felt filled with shame, yet she was also wondering when she could next go through and eat some more of that glorious meat. Something about its dead, cold feel seemed so much more enticing than any rabbit meat.

"And could you fetch some rags from just past the back door?" Fanny asked, before glancing at the pot as it was set down. "Well done. That's the one I would have chosen myself."

"Thank you," Rebecca said, almost ashamed now to look the other woman in the eye as she hurried to the door and pulled it open. "I'm sorry. I'll just be a moment and -"

Before she could get another word out, she froze in the doorway as she saw Oliver sitting on the ground outside, with his back resting against the wall. In that moment, her eyes widened with shock as she saw his pale, dead face, and after a few seconds she could only scream.

CHAPTER FIFTEEN

"IT MUST HAVE BEEN infected," Fanny said calmly, standing in the study, where Oliver's body had been laid out on one of the desks. "I should hope that his passing was at least quick."

She paused, before pulling a stretch of fabric up and over her dead husband's face.

"Mrs. Baxter," Richard said, "Fanny, I... I do not know what to say. You were married for many years, were you not?"

"Many indeed," she replied softly. "He was a good man. Despite my many complaints over time, a woman could not have asked for a more dependable husband. He was good with his hands, always very good at fixing things and..."

Her voice trailed off, and after a few seconds she reached up and wiped a solitary tear from the corner of one eye.

"I shall miss him very much," she continued, "and I shall make sure that he receives a proper burial. I cannot afford much, but what I have I -"

"I shall of course cover any such costs," Richard told her. "There is a very fine cemetery in the village, and I am sure I can speak to the priest and have a spot found."

"Oliver was a common man," Fanny replied, turning to him. "It hardly seems right that after a life like the one he lived, he should suddenly be buried as if he had been rich."

"You do not want him to go into the cemetery?"

"I think..."

She paused, as if she was giving the matter much thought.

"I shall make arrangements," Richard told her, "and you can think about it. We will of course do whatever you wish. I just hope you know that I appreciated Oliver very much and came to care about him a great deal. I saw him almost as an equal."

"You should not say such things," she replied. "You are a great man, Sir."

"As was Oliver," he said firmly, "in his own way. I truly do believe that I must do the right thing by him in death, but I shall of course be guided by your wishes. And I trust that you know you have a home here with my family for life. If I might be so bold, Mrs. Baxter, I would even go so far as to say that you are *part* of that family."

"You are too kind," she told him. "Mr. Hadlow, I would like to return to my work in the kitchen. The meal can still be saved if I attend to things swiftly. Meanwhile, I believe you have another matter that requires your urgent attention."

"Of course," he replied. "I shall endeavor to contact a priest."

"While that is a worthy cause," she said, "I was referring to something else. Sir, do you not think that there is someone else here in this house who requires your care?"

***

"Did you see his eyes?" Rebecca whispered, still sitting in the dining room and staring ahead into the darkness as candles flickered nearby. "It's as if the poor man died of fright."

"I think we can safely say," Richard replied, "that he lost too much blood to live. Mrs. Baxter also believes that he suffered from an infection, which is hardly surprising given the nature of his injury. I myself inspected that saw and its teeth are beyond repair."

"But he seemed to have died while looking

at something," she continued, before turning to him. "Don't you think so? Didn't it seem that way to you as well?"

"I think that in the moment of death, any man might easily be gripped by great fear."

"He was acting strangely in the night," she told him. "I didn't mention it this morning, because I didn't want to cause any concern, but during the night I followed him outside and saw him clearing a space on the ground. He told me that..."

She hesitated, suddenly aware that her husband might not want her to broach the subject of the previous Mrs. Hadlow.

"He said some strange things," she said cautiously, "and he seemed generally fearful."

"Then that confirms the fever," he replied, "at least as far as I'm concerned. Oliver Baxter was a good man with a solid mind. He would never ordinarily talk about anything irrational, nor would he go creeping about in the dead of night. If that's what happened, then clearly he was in the grip of some awful change to his constitution." He reached over and placed a hand on her knee. "There can be little doubt about the matter now."

"But what if he saw... someone?" she asked. "Or something?"

"There would be nothing to see."

"He dug a cross up from the ground," she continued. "A crucifix."

"If he became superstitious at the end, that only shows that he knew his own death was approaching. People do that, you know. I myself have been with people who are nearing their demise, and they can come out with the most astonishing claims. Rebecca, have you ever been around death?"

She paused, before shaking her head.

"Then take this from someone with experience," he continued. "There is little use in searching for logic or reason in the actions of a dying man, for you shall most likely find none. What's important is that you put these concerns out of your mind and try to focus on the land of the living. You have endured a difficult start to your time here at the house, but things will improve rapidly, I'm sure. And soon we shall be able to start creating our own little family here." He squeezed her knee gently. "You are my wife," he added, "and I shall expect to treat you as such."

"Of course," she said softly, even though she wasn't entirely sure what he meant.

Hearing a tapping sound, she turned and looked at the window. Rain had been threatening to arrive all day, coming and going but never developing beyond a light drizzle, yet now – as darkness fell outside – the weather seemed to be on the turn; rain was falling with greater intensity, and a moment later Rebecca noticed another drip making its way through the window's frame.

"Mrs. Baxter has everything in hand in the kitchen," Richard told her. "I think that after all this difficulty, tomorrow we should try to turn a fresh page. Do you think you can do that?"

"Anything for you," she replied, before forcing a smile.

"I must go and attend to a few matters," he said, getting to his feet. "Will you be alright here?"

She nodded, but then – as she watched him heading out of the room – she was suddenly gripped by fresh concern.

"Richard?"

He stopped and turn to her.

"Richard," she continued, "have you ever felt something... inside you... some urge or need... that you considered to be wrong?"

He hesitated for a moment, before furrowing his brow.

"Whatever do you mean?" he asked.

Before she could answer, she thought back to the sensation of human meat in her mouth. She had no idea why she had felt so compelled to tear strips from Oliver's amputated arm; the idea seemed ghastly now, yet she wondered whether she would be overcome once more by that desire if she returned to the storage room. She desperately wanted to ask someone for advice, for she wondered whether her urge had in fact been quite normal, but deep down she worried that she was almost becoming some kind of monster.

"Rebecca?" Richard continued. "Is something wrong?"

"No," she lied, feeling all her courage slipping away. "No, I was just thinking out loud about certain things. There's absolutely nothing to worry about."

As those words left her mouth, the rain began to batter the window even faster, tapping relentlessly now against the glass panes.

"Things will get better," Richard told her. "I promise. This is going to be a happy house, because I will accept no other outcome. And one day, I assure you, we shall look back upon these moments and merely be thankful that we have been able to get through the darkness. You understand what I'm saying to you, Rebecca, do you not?"

"I think so," she replied, "and I must thank you for putting my mind at ease. My father always told me that as a woman, I am likely to think insensible thoughts from time to time. I am so relieved to know that I have a husband who is able to calm me down and set me straight." She took a deep breath, attempting to reset her composure. "As you say, these things will pass and this shall become a happy house."

"It shall," he said firmly. "I simply refuse to countenance any other option."

AMY CROSS

CHAPTER SIXTEEN

RAIN AND WIND BATTERED the window, causing the glass panes to rattle loudly as Rebecca lay wide awake in bed. She had scarcely even closed her eyes since retiring, and while Richard lay sleeping soundly alongside her she could only stare up once again at the ceiling.

Wind was whistling through the eaves, bringing the house almost to life, causing all manner of creaks and groans. Rebecca had thought that a new house would be better able to withstand the onslaught of some bad weather, but instead she found herself wondering whether the entire place might yet blow away. Yet, in truth, this cacophony was not the cause of her wakefulness.

In her belly, a biting hunger was clawing at her guts, demanding sustenance.

Finally, sitting up, Rebecca realized that Oliver's arm was most likely still in the storage room, but that another source existed now, one that might taste fresher and more succulent. She knew that Richard and Fanny had laid Oliver's corpse out in the room to the side of the study, ready to take it into the village the following day; she herself had not gone through to see the corpse, but now she found herself imagining the red, moist flesh that was going to waste down there. She told herself that she must show some restraint, yet at that moment a fresh burst of pain filled her gut and she somehow understood that only meat would calm her body.

Although she knew that Richard would be horrified, she carefully climbed out of bed and crept across the room, and then she made her way out onto the landing. This time she was wearing only her nightdress, having not even stopped to cover herself with a gown.

Once she was sure that nobody else was up, she hurried down the stairs, going as quickly as possible while taking care to make little noise. A few of the steps let out small bumping sounds under the pressure of her bare feet, but Rebecca soon reached the hallway and crept through to the study. She told herself that she only needed a few morsels of the man's flesh to calm the pain in her belly, and that then once daylight arrived she would be able to find some way to stop these cravings forever.

She stopped and listened to the gentle bumps and groans of the house, and then she stepped into the study. As she was about to head to the door at the far end, she stopped as she saw a crucifix resting propped against the wall. She stared at the shape, confused by its presence, and then as she stepped closer she realized that it was the same crucifix that Oliver had taken from the grave outside. Confused about how it had ended up inside, she reached out to touch the object, although she held back at the last second.

As she tried to work out what to do next, she stood in the cold study and felt a shiver run through her bones.

"I must make haste," she whispered finally, turning and heading to the door in the corner.

She reached for the handle, only to stop as soon as she heard a heavy scraping sound coming from somewhere over her shoulder. She froze for a moment, terrified that either Richard or Fanny might have caught her, and then she turned to look back.

Relieved, she saw that there was no-one else in the moonlit room. She waited, just to be sure, yet slowly she felt a sense of dread starting to fill her body. That scraping sound had most certainly been real, and now she wondered whether she was being watched. As hard as she tried to convince herself otherwise, she felt certain now that a pair of eyes must be glaring directly at her, and the sensation only grew with each passing second until she felt as if she might be about to call out for help.

A moment later, reminding herself that she was not supposed to be up and about in the first place, she managed to get her fears under control. There was quite clearly nobody lurking anywhere nearby in the room, for there was certainly enough moonlight to pick out any person.

And then, just as she was about to turn away, she saw what appeared to be a dark crucifix floating in mid-air just a few feet from her face. She stared, wondering how such a thing could seemingly be holding itself aloft, and then she looked to her left and saw that the crucifix she'd noticed earlier was missing. She turned to the object hanging in the air, and in that moment she understood that the scraping sound must have been -

Suddenly the crucifix turned and rushed at her. Rebecca held her hands up and screamed, but she was a fraction of a second too late and the crucifix's side hit her on the cheek, cutting her just below the eye as she fell back and then slumped down onto the floor. As the metal crucifix landed next to her with a loud thud, Rebecca pulled into the corner and kept her hands up, terrified that someone was about to strike her again.

A single bead of blood ran down from the wound on her cheek.

"Who's there?" she stammered, filled with fear now. "Show... show yourself!"

She waited, and a moment later she heard footsteps rushing down the stairs. Turning to look over at the open doorway, she was just in time to see a figure stepping into view. The figure hurried away again, before returning with a candle, the light of which revealed his face.

"Rebecca?" Richard said. "What's happening down here?"

"I..."

Reaching up, she wiped the blood from her face, before looking over at the crucifix on the floor. For a moment she was too gripped by fear to answer, but after a few seconds she turned to Richard and he knelt next to her.

"You're hurt," he pointed out.

"It's nothing."

"I heard a cry," he continued. "Rebecca, what are you doing up in the middle of the night? And why do you not have a candle with you?"

"I just came down for -"

Stopping herself just in time, she realized that she could never reveal the reason for her trip downstairs. She looked at the crucifix again, but she worried that mentioning exactly what had happened might only make her seem to have lost her senses. The pain in her belly was gone, most likely chased away by sheer panic, and after a few more seconds she began to sit up. Another bead of blood ran down her cheek, but she wiped it away quickly and told herself that she merely needed to return to the bedroom.

"I'm fine," she said, although she knew that she did not sound particularly convincing. "I just..."

Realizing that the pain in her head had returned, she slowly got to her feet. She felt a little unsteady, but she put this down to her general state of confusion.

"I think I just need to sleep," she continued, as she heard more footsteps and saw Fanny stepping into the doorway. "I'm so sorry to have woken you both like this. I never wanted cause any kind if disturbance."

"What is happening down here?" Fanny asked, and she too was holding a candle.

"Just some foolishness on my part," Rebecca said, and now she was on her feet she stepped past Richard and headed toward the door. "Really, I just want to go to bed and -"

Stopping suddenly, she looked past Fanny and saw another figure out in the hallway. This figure was shrouded in darkness, yet Rebecca could tell that she was seeing a woman. Opening her mouth to ask who else was in the house, she held back at the last second, telling herself that she was merely misinterpreting a shadow. And then, tilting her head slightly, she realized that this supposed shadow was most certainly in the shape of a person.

"Who are you?" she whispered.

"What is that doing here?" Fanny asked, suddenly pushing past her and hurrying across the room.

Blinking, Rebecca saw that the figure in the hallway was suddenly gone. A moment later she felt a hand on her arm, and she turned to find Fanny glaring at her while holding the crucifix.

"What is this doing in the house?" the older woman barked. "Girl, you will tell me at once!"

"I -"

"Why is it here?" Fanny shouted.

"Mr. Baxter brought it in!"

"Liar!"

"I swear, he -"

In that moment, Fanny slapped her hard across the side of the face, with enough force to make her instinctively step back. Raising her hand, Rebecca felt a stinging pain as she stared in shock at the anger on Fanny's face.

"Why did you bring this thing inside?" Fanny sneered. "Why did you remove it from its rightful place?"

"I didn't!" Rebecca sobbed, before turning to Richard. "I swear! Please, you both have to believe me, it was Mr. Baxter who brought that thing inside! At least, I think it was, I didn't see it again after he took it from the grave outside!"

"He would never do such a thing," Fanny told her, before turning and looking toward the window. "Would he? Was he really such a fool that he'd interfere like that?"

"What is going on here?" Richard asked. "I think both of you need to sit down and speak reasonably about whatever events have transpired here."

"It might not be too late," Fanny stammered, evidently having not heard him at all. She hesitated, before carrying the crucifix out of the room, hurrying across the hallway. "I might still have a chance to put it back!"

"What is this madness?" Richard said, turning to Rebecca. "Can somebody please tell me what is going on in my own home?"

CHAPTER SEVENTEEN

RAIN WAS LASHING DOWN now as Fanny – wearing a gown over her nightdress – hurried out from the front door and made her way across the garden. In her right hand, she was holding the crucifix she'd brought from inside, and she was muttering away to herself as she rushed through the cold night air.

A few seconds later, Richard and Rebecca reached the doorway, although they both stopped before stepping outside. Richard held up his candle, although its light was powerless against the night's all-encompassing darkness.

"Where's she going?" Rebecca asked, although deep down she already knew the answer to that question.

"The woman has quite lost her mind,"

Richard replied. "The anguish of losing her husband must have tipped her into utter insanity."

"We should go to her."

Stepping forward, Rebecca felt rain falling against her face just as Richard grabbed her arm to hold her back.

"Wait here," he said firmly. "I should like to deal with this situation myself. There is no need for you to be further inconvenienced."

Although she desperately wanted to help Fanny, Rebecca did as she was told. Stepping back into the doorway, she watched helplessly as her husband made his way out into the rain. As he hurried through the darkness, Rebecca looked ahead and saw that Fanny had already dropped to her knees in front of the grave, just a few feet from the foot of the old oak tree. Wind was blowing more and more rain through the night air, and Rebecca felt powerless as she saw Richard stopping next to Fanny and trying to pull her up.

"Can't this madness end?" Rebecca whispered. "Why -"

Before she could finish, she saw that a third figure was over by the tree. She was unable to make out any details, but the silhouette of a woman was standing behind Richard, who seemed completely unaware of this presence.

"Richard!" Rebecca shouted, waving at him frantically. "There's someone with you!"

She waited, but she immediately knew that she hadn't been heard. She hesitated, wondering what to do next, before setting out across the garden herself. She hated the idea that she was going against her husband's strict instructions, yet she also knew that he had to be warned about this strange presence that had now shown itself multiple times. As she got closer to the tree, she heard Richard still trying to reason with Fanny, while the older woman sobbed hysterically on the ground and tried desperately to push the crucifix back down into the mud.

"You are acting beyond reason," Richard said as Rebecca reached them. "There is a limit to my tolerance."

"There's something here!" Rebecca gasped, looking around but no longer seeing the strange woman. "Richard, there's someone else here with us!"

"I told you to wait inside," he said firmly, before pulling again on Fanny's arm. "I really must insist that we all return to the house at once. I will not allow madness to take root, for once it takes root -"

"There might still be time!" Fanny sobbed desperately. "How long was it away for? Twenty-four hours? There might still be a chance to keep her down there!"

"Woman," Richard replied, "you are

becoming hysterical."

"Damn you, Oliver!" Fanny cried. "What could possibly have possessed you?"

Looking around once more, Rebecca still saw no sign of the other woman, yet she felt more and more certain that some ghostly presence was nearby. She knew that Catherine Hadlow had died earlier in the year, and she knew that the poor woman had been the victim of some horrible accident at the house, but she had never managed to uncover too many of the details. She'd told herself over and over again that she didn't need to know too much about Richard's first wife, yet now she worried that some preternatural event might be overtaking the house and all of its inhabitants. She couldn't help looking around again and again, terrified that at any moment she might find the face of a dead woman staring back at her.

"Do you think it's too late?" Fanny whimpered, still on the ground. "Please, say that it's not! I couldn't handle thinking that I might have to face her again!"

"Are you coming inside," Richard said firmly, "or must I leave you out here to die of the cold? My earlier promises to you notwithstanding, Mrs. Baxter, I have my limits and you are pushing them exceedingly far on this night."

"There," Fanny replied, pulling back and falling against the dirt, then pointing at the spot where the crucifix lay almost entirely re-submerged in the mud. "It is done! That must surely hold her back, as it has held her back for all these months!"

"We should go inside," Rebecca said, turning to her husband. "Richard, I know you do not wish to hear such things, but I fear that some terrible spirit is afoot!"

"The madness is catching," he muttered angrily, before grabbing Fanny's other arm and forcing her up onto her feet. "I will tolerate it no longer! We are all going inside, and that is the end of the matter!"

***

Rebecca watched as the candle began to burn, and then she used it to light two more. Once she had set all three of the candles in place on the table, she turned and looked across the study.

Fanny was still slumped in the chair in the far corner, breathing heavily as she kept one hand across her face. The sight was somewhat surreal for Rebecca, since until that moment she had always considered Fanny to be one of the strongest women she had ever met in her life. Now, however, Fanny seemed to have entirely broken down, as if she could no longer accept reality.

Hearing footsteps, Rebecca turned just as Richard walked across the hallway and into the house's front room. After glancing at Fanny again, to make sure that she was unlikely to throw herself from the chair, she hurried out and through to the next room, where her husband was warming himself against a fire in the hearth. The thunderous expression on his face made clear that he was not happy.

"She is resting," Rebecca said cautiously, although she immediately realized that this might not be the correct way to explain Fanny's present condition. "In a way," she added. "She is better than before, at least."

"I should have known that this would happen," Richard told her. "A woman is bound by her very nature to suffer like this when her husband dies. I thought Mrs. Baxter might be more resistant than the average woman, yet that has turned out to not be the case at all."

He let out a heavy sigh.

"I am starting to think," he added, "that it might be better after all if she were to leave this place. Once her husband has been given a good burial, that is."

"Do you think that everything she has said is untrue?"

Rebecca looked over her shoulder, to make sure that there was no sign of Fanny stirring, and then she turned to her husband again.

"Richard," she continued cautiously, "I must

speak to you of things that might be... discomforting. I have refrained from asking too much about the first Mrs. Hadlow, about Catherine, but I feel that now I need to know exactly what happened to her."

"There was an accident. The details are not important."

"But they might be," she said, taking a step forward. She worried that she was challenging her husband's authority, yet she had to know the truth. "I know she died here, and that she was buried here as well. Did you not give consideration to having her buried in a churchyard?"

"I have plans to have the ground here consecrated," he told her. "Next year, I shall have a small chapel built on this land, and then Catherine's resting place will be more respectable."

"But -"

"Great families do such things, you know," he added, turning to her. "They have mausoleums and suchlike on their land, in the grounds of their houses. I wish to have the same." He paused for a moment. "There is no reason why Hadlow House should be any less grand than the homes of those who spit upon the name of my family. I will be their equal!"

"I understand," she replied, although this was only half-true. "Nevertheless, might it not have been wise to have her buried in a churchyard first, and then move her here?"

"Moving her would have been disrespectful," he argued. "Rebecca, I made my decision and it was the correct one. Do not challenge me on it."

"I am sorry." She thought for a moment, trying to work out how else she might get at the truth. "Richard," she added, "can you think of any other reason why Catherine might, in death, seek vengeance? Can you think of any reason why she might not be resting in peace?"

"You are speaking of things you do not comprehend," he said darkly.

"I have seen her," she replied. "God help me, I wish it were not true, but I have seen her and I think I even felt her touch when first I was in your bed upstairs. It was shortly after I was thrown from the carriage, down into the water, and someone entered the room unseen by me. It was not you, nor was it Mr. or Mrs. Baxter. I have come to believe that there is only one other candidate."

She waited for an answer, but Richard remained silent and she began to wonder whether she might be getting through to him. At the same time, she could only begin to imagine the agony that he must be feeling at the thought of his dead wife returning to the world. Making her way over to him, she placed a hand on the small of his back and watched the side of his face, and she felt her heart break for his suffering.

"If she is here," she said after a moment, "then is it not our duty to find out why, and to try to help her? Should we not attempt to uncover the source of her pain?"

Again she waited, hoping against hope that he might agree.

"I fear to disturb such things," he told her finally. "To meddle with the darkness of death. Might we not simply wait and hope that this all turns out to be a nightmare? Might -"

He froze for a few seconds, as if he was too scared to even complete that sentence.

"I do not want to know that such things are even possible," he added, his voice trembling with fear. "I just do not want to be aware. I would rather live the rest of my life with my eyes closed to such things and -"

Suddenly a scream rang out, and they both turned to look across the hallway as Fanny's agonized cry rang out from the study.

.

CHAPTER EIGHTEEN

"WHATEVER HAS POSSESSED YOU?" Richard shouted as he stormed through into the next room. "Have you entirely taken leave of your senses?"

"She's coming for us!" Fanny gasped, still sitting in the chair but gripping the arms as if her entire body had stiffened. "That fool released her spirit from the grave and now she's coming for us all!"

"Woman, you surprise me tonight," Richard replied, marching over to her. "You have gone from the wisest woman I know to the most foolish on the planet!"

"She was at the window just now," Fanny sobbed, as tears streamed down her face. She turned and looked at the window that ran along one of the walls. "She wanted me to see her. There is nothing to stop her coming inside now, but I am sure she means to frighten the life from us first."

"Are you sure it was her?" Rebecca asked, hurrying to the window and trying to peer out at the darkness. "Could you be mistaken?"

"I saw her face," Fanny replied through gritted teeth. "All hope is lost. She is returning from the grave to make us all pay for what happened to her."

"What happened to her was an accident," Richard said firmly.

Fanny hesitated, before looking up at him.

"She fell," he continued. "That's all. You arrived shortly after it all transpired, but I was there and I saw it all. She fell and was pierced by one of those infernal rods of metal, and nothing could have been done to save her. She died on the ground, right before me, with most of her blood having soaked deep into the soil beneath the house in which we now stand." He paused, watching Fanny's face intently as if he was scrutinizing her reaction with great keenness. "And then she was buried," he added, "and that is the end of it. You are a woman of faith, Fanny, and I have always admired that about you. If you search your heart, you must realize that there is no way Catherine could possibly have returned."

"I don't see anyone," Rebecca said, cupping her hands around her eyes as she continued to look outside. Rain was battering the window now, crashing down through the darkness. "It's so difficult, though. I can see almost nothing at all. For all I know, she could be there."

"This madness is contagious," Richard muttered, before turning and walking out of the room, his footsteps banging loudly against the wooden boards.

"There is no way to fight against her," Fanny whimpered in the chair. "We are all lost."

Rebecca turned to her.

"There are no secrets to be kept from the dead," Fanny continued. "They know all that we have done. All our sins. They see into our hearts and find the darkness."

"Why are you so afraid of her?" Rebecca asked. "Was she really such a fearful woman?"

"She was a *good* woman," Fanny explained, "and she might well have lived a long and happy life here at Mr. Hadlow's house, were it for that awful accident that befell her when she arrived."

"But if it was an accident," Rebecca continued, "then why is she angry?"

She waited, before taking a few steps across the room. She could hear Richard hurrying upstairs now.

"Mrs. Baxter?" she continued, as wind and rain continued to batter the window behind her. "Why might the spirit of Catherine Hadlow feel wronged?"

She waited for an answer, but a moment later the banging of the window panes began to change somewhat, become almost a kind of incessant tapping sound. Realizing that this sounded as if somebody was indeed outside, as if some soul was attempting to attract attention, Rebecca slowly turned and looked back at the window. She could still see nothing outside, of course, yet deep down she wondered whether some hidden figure might be lurking in the darkness and tapping gently on the glass.

Suddenly a shot rang out from somewhere upstairs.

"What was that?" Rebecca gasped, looking up at the ceiling.

A moment later, hearing footsteps storming down the stairs, she turned just in time to see Richard hurrying back into the room with some kind of pistol.

"What are you doing with that?" she asked, watching as he stopped and examined the weapon.

Richard muttered something under his breath.

"Richard, what is your purpose with that?" she continued, stepping closer. "What do you mean to do?"

"When a dog is mad," he replied, examining the pistol more closely, "it is only fair to put it down. I believe the same mercy should be extended to people. I thought I saw something in one of the bedrooms. I discharged a shot but I succeeded only in damaging the wall above the fireplace."

Rebecca hesitated, before looking at Fanny and seeing that the older woman was now sobbing frantically in the chair, with her hands covering her eyes.

"You cannot mean that," Rebecca hissed, hurrying to Richard and putting a hand on his arm. "Richard, the poor woman is out of her mind after the death of her husband. You said it yourself, it is only natural that she should suffer. You cannot intend to do her harm."

"Her mind is broken and I fear it will never be repaired," he told her.

"She just needs time." She paused, before squeezing his arm a little. "This night is horrendous for her soul. Give her until morning and I am sure she will be calmer."

He hesitated, before setting the pistol down.

"If you are wrong," he said cautiously, "then her agony is only extended. I fear that her mind will never recover and we are only delaying the inevitable."

"You cannot end her life as if she is some stray animal," she reminded him. "Richard, why do you rush to act in this way? Is there some other reason why you do not want to hear her speak of...

of your earlier wife?" She immediately worried that she had done wrong by even hinting at Catherine's existence, yet at the same time she knew she could not live forever without knowing the truth. And the more she watched her husband's face now, the more she felt that he was hiding from something. "You can tell me," she continued. "I want to know."

"Catherine...."

His voice trailed off.

"Yes?" Rebecca whispered.

"I fear," he continued, "that..."

"She is here," Fanny said suddenly, and Richard and Rebecca both turned to see that she was now standing and staring toward the hallway. "She is in the house. Now that she is fully freed from her grave, she is held back by nothing. She can come and go as she pleases, and she lingers only because she wants to torture us." At that moment, one floorboard creaked loudly in the hallway. "She knows exactly what she is doing," Fanny continued. "She knows how to make us suffer. You saw the fear in Oliver's eyes. She is going to do the same to us."

Richard reached again for the pistol, only for Rebecca to take his hand, keeping him from picking the weapon up.

"We only did what we did," Fanny continued, "because we believed it to be right."

Rebecca turned to her.

"You have to understand," Fanny added, "that we had little time in which to make a decision. So little time. And we are but fallible people. God-fearing, of course, but fallible. And in that moment, we chose to ease the burden of the living, Mr. Baxter, and we did so because we had good hearts. I just wish that Catherine could see that, and that she could understand why we did what we did."

"What did you do?" Rebecca whispered.

"We made the right decision," Fanny said firmly, even as tears streamed down her face, "and I would do exactly the same thing again."

"What did you do?" Rebecca asked again.

"It must be so easy for you," Fanny continued bitterly, "who have no experience of the world. You can criticize others, but I know in my heart that Oliver and I made the right choice. Catherine could not be allowed to live!"

"But what did you do?" Rebecca asked.

"Yes," Richard said, stepping past her, approaching Fanny cautiously. "I have trusted you, Frances Baxter, and I still do, but you are giving me great cause for concern. I would know right now if there is any stain, no matter how small, on your soul."

"There is no stain, Sir," Fanny replied, as a door out in the hallway began to creak open in the darkness. "Only the divine light that comes from knowing that one has made the right choice in the eyes of the Lord."

"What did you do?" he sneered firmly. "You will tell me, or – regardless of my wife's preference – I will fetch my pistol immediately."

"We did what we had to do," she replied, staring up at him with tears glistening in her eyes. "We did what anyone with God in their hearts would have done in such a moment. We made sure, Sir, that your desire for a happy home would not become undone."

CHAPTER NINETEEN

January 1689...

"THERE WILL BE MUCH to do," Fanny muttered darkly, as she and Oliver rode their horses through the forest, approaching the clearing up ahead. "Mr. Hadlow will want everything to be perfect, that is for sure. And we must oblige."

"My back has been bad of late," Oliver replied. "I fear it might slow me down."

"You must not let it," she told him, as she spotted several workmen in the clearing. "There is..."

Before she could finish, she realized that something was wrong. At first she wasn't able to determine *why* she felt this way, merely that some secret extra sense was tingling; she saw two horses tied to a nearby stake, but after a few seconds she realized that the workmen were all standing idly by, looking down into the pit they had dug as if they were struck motionless by some awful sight. And as she and Oliver made their way ever closer, Fanny realized that a strange silence had fallen upon the clearing.

"This is a strange sight," Oliver murmured.

"Something is wrong," Fanny said, bringing her horse to a halt and immediately dismounting, before hurrying to the edge of the pit. "I fear -"

Stopping suddenly, she saw the horrific sight. Richard Hadlow was kneeling on the ground, tending to his new wife Catherine, whose dead face was turned to look up at the gray sky. Blood had soaked the front of the woman's dress, and Fanny quickly saw that some kind of metal protrusion had burst through her chest, impaling her and leaving her dead on the ground. Indeed, as she tried to comprehend exactly how this turn of events could have transpired, Fanny realized that the ground beneath Catherine's body was darker than the rest, as if the woman's blood had flowed into the soil.

"She is dead," Richard said, his voice tense with sorrow. "It happened barely half an hour ago, Mrs. Baxter. A terrible accident has taken her from me mere days after..."

His voice trailed off.

"She was to be the mother of my children,"

he continued. "This house was to be the happiest of homes. I saw it so often in my mind, and I worked so hard to make it a reality... and then one awful accident has ripped it all away. I fear the Hadlow name has become a curse for all who come near it."

"May the Lord have mercy on her poor soul," Fanny whispered, shocked by the sight of the dead woman's face. "It was but two days ago that she and I talked last, and she was making such happy plans for the future."

"I was a fool to think I could do any of this," Richard sobbed. "A wretched, contemptible fool. I only wish that I had been the one to pay the price, instead of this poor woman."

Fanny hesitated for a moment, before starting to clamber down into the pit. Ignoring Oliver's attempts to help, she dropped into the mud and – ignoring the fact that the hem of her skirt was trailing in the mud – she picked her way over to her employer and dropped to her knees. Reaching out, she took hold of the side of his face and forced him to turn and look at her directly.

"You are not to give up, Sir," she said firmly, glancing briefly at the dead woman's closed eyes before turning to Richard again. "You are too good a man to do that."

"But -"

"We shall make this good," she added, before he could finish, "and then you shall find yourself another wife. Is that understood? All might seem lost now, but I promise you... I will not let you surrender to fate."

***

A few hours later, with his back singing with pain, Oliver stepped back and let his shovel fall to the ground. Wiping sweat from his brow, he admired the grave he had dug next to the old oak tree at the far end of the garden.

"Is it ready?" Fanny called out keenly. "Oliver, are you done?"

"As done as I might ever be," he replied wearily, looking at the thick tree roots that remained knotted at one end of the grave. "I can't cut through those, they're too thick. Unless you want me to extend the grave, I -"

"There'll be no need for that," Fanny said, interrupting him as she carried Catherine's corpse to the edge in a large cloth sack and began to lower it down. "Here, take her. Now that Mr. Hadlow has gone on ahead to the village, we do not have much time. I must catch up to him before sundown and make sure that he retains his hope."

Struggling a little with the weight of the dead woman, Oliver nevertheless managed to lower her down and set her gently at the bottom of the pit, although her head initially bumped against some of the tree roots.

"Isn't it a little wrong to bury her here?" he asked.

"She has no family to speak of," Fanny replied a little breathlessly, "and Mr. Hadlow intends to build a chapel on this site. He spoke earlier of wanting to give her a proper burial, but I am sure that once he has a new wife he will barely think of this one." She paused for a moment. "In truth, Mr. Hadlow was married to Catherine for such a short period of time, I am not even sure that it counts as a marriage at all. Indeed, I am confident that over time she will be swiftly forgotten. Now, Oliver, let us waste no more time. Fill in this grave."

Sighing, Oliver turned to grab his shovel, but at the last second he froze as he heard a faint groan coming from nearby. Looking over his shoulder, he saw Catherine's body resting in the sack; a moment later, to his horror, the sack moved slightly and the groan returned.

"Fanny?" he stammered, as fear spread through his chest.

"Have you got started yet?" she called back to him, having already made her way from the pit's edge.

"Fanny, get back here," he said as the sack continued to move slightly. "Fanny, I think we might all have overlooked one matter."

"What is it?" she hissed, hurrying back to the edge. "Those workmen have wandered half a mile away. I must get them back here and set them to work again so that -"

Stopping suddenly, she too saw that there were signs of life coming from inside the sack. She stared for a few seconds, scarcely able to believe what was happening, and then she clambered down into the pit and stood alongside her husband.

"Do my eyes deceive me?" Oliver asked. "Fanny, please, tell me that I am wrong..."

Fanny hesitated, before stepping around the slowly shifting corpse and reaching down. Reaching down, she pulled the top of the sack aside, and she let out a shocked gasp as she saw Catherine's open eyes staring back up at her.

"Please," Catherine whispered, "I do not know... what is happening to me?"

"You had an accident," Fanny stammered. "We all thought..."

Her voice trailed off as she tried to make sense of what she was seeing.

"Where am I?" Catherine asked, turning to look around the grave. After a moment she spotted the huge tree roots that comprised the grave's nearest wall. "Where is Richard? Mrs. Baxter, I do not fell well." Reaching down, she touched the wound on her belly.

"It is a miracle, to be sure," Oliver said. "I

suppose one might survive such a thing, but one would need to have been watched over by the angels themselves."

"I feel so strange," Catherine whispered, and now she was starting to panic a little. "I remember falling, and then... I think I screamed, and then... I remember nothing after that. Mrs. Baxter, I'm scared, where is Richard? Please, can you tell me what happened?"

"We must get her out and find a doctor at once," Oliver told his wife, before waiting for her response. "Fanny? By the Lord's grace, there is still time to save her!"

Fanny opened her mouth to reply, before hesitating for a moment.

"The metal pierced her belly, to be sure," she whispered finally. "She will never be able to give Master Richard the family he so keenly desires. Indeed, it is far from certain that she will live a normal life at all, even in the unlikely event that she makes a recovery."

"But we must get her to a doctor," Oliver reminded her. "Fanny, there is no time to waste. We must get her onto one of the horses, or perhaps someone has a cart we can borrow." Again he waited, and again Fanny seemed frozen in place. "Fanny, time is of the essence."

Fanny hesitated for a few seconds, before reaching over and slowly taking the shovel from his hand. He resisted slightly, but only for a moment, and then he watched as his wife loaded the shovel's tip with a pile of dirt.

"Fanny?" he said cautiously. "What do you mean to do here?"

"Mr. Hadlow can find another wife," she told him, as Catherine whimpered on the ground. "One who can give him a family. One who can make him happy. This one..." She looked down at Catherine's tear-filled eyes. "This one can do neither," she added. "Not now. Yet Mr. Hadlow is too good a man to make such a decision. So it must be made for him."

With that, she shoveled dirt onto Catherine's face, smothering the poor woman's cries even as she tried desperately to wriggle free from the sack.

CHAPTER TWENTY

Nine months later...

"SAY IT TO ME plainly," Richard said, as bad weather continued to batter the house and the candles flickered nearby. "Do you mean to tell me that when you buried Catherine..."

"She was still alive?" Rebecca whispered, her eyes open wide with shock.

"Do you remember what I told you after that awful day?" Fanny asked her master. "You were on the verge of surrendering all your hope, but I sat you down and told you that Catherine would not want you to give up hope. I told you that you are a good man and that you must stay true to what you know is your true calling."

"Fanny," Richard replied, "please tell me

that I misconstrue your meaning."

"She was no good," she continued, "not after her injury. And besides, she would almost certainly never have survived the journey to find a doctor. She had by some miracle clung to life until that moment, but the idea of her long-term survival was simply not credible. You must understand that I saved us all a great deal of trouble, by avoiding the desperate hopeless scrambled to save her life. You saw her injury, Mr. Baxter! You know she could never have given you a child!"

"Fanny," he said again, "I thought that when you buried Catherine, she was dead."

"She might as well have been," she sneered. "Besides, I worked quickly. Oliver could not bring himself to do the deed, so I filled the grave in and I am quite sure that she would have been dead by the time I was finished. I know the manner of her dispatch was unusual, but all things considered it was fairly quick and painless. When a dog is dying, one must put it out of its misery. I know you understand that, Mr. Hadlow, so please try to understand why Oliver and I did what we did. The only reason I didn't tell you was that I know you have a good heart, and I worried you might struggle with the knowledge."

Stepping forward, she put her hands on his chest.

"Mr. Hadlow," she continued, "everything I

have ever done has been for the betterment of your life. I have never wavered in my determination to serve you!"

The panes in the window shuddered again, almost like thunder.

"This foul act must be undone," Richard said after a moment. "When I married Catherine, I promised to take care of her, and instead I allowed her to die in this awful manner. I must fulfill my promise."

"You have another wife now," Fanny reminded him, before pointing at Rebecca. "She is strong, and she can carry your child! You must see that things have worked out for the best!" She hesitated, before looking out into the hallway and letting out a gasp as she spotted the faintest hint of Catherine's silhouette in the shadows. "And that foolish woman," she sneered, "must understand that – fairly or not – her chance is gone."

"This must be undone," Richard stammered, pushing Fanny away and then storming out of the room. "Now!"

***

"Richard!"

Hurrying through the darkness, with rain lashing down, Rebecca finally stopped as she saw that her husband had taken a shovel to the grave and had already managed to get a long way down. He was digging furiously, throwing mud aside as he tried to get down to Catherine's corpse. Rebecca watched for a moment, worried that any attempt to disturb him might earn his anger, but after a few seconds – soaked to the skin now as rain continued to fall – she wiped some hair from across her face and took one more step forward.

"Richard," she continued, raising her voice a little in an attempt to be heard over the sound of so much bad weather, "what are you doing?"

"What does it look like I'm doing?" he asked breathlessly.

"It looks like you're disturbing the last resting place of this poor soul," she pointed out. "Richard, whatever horrors occurred at the end of her life, I'm not sure that this is the proper way to put it right."

"She should be buried properly."

"So arrange that first," she continued. "Have a fitting grave ready and waiting so that she can be transferred, instead of digging her up in a fit of rage."

"I will not be lectured by a woman," he replied, before slipping slightly on the muddy ground. "Curse this rain!"

"Richard -"

"You do not need to be here!" he roared. "I have been patient with you up until this point,

Rebecca, but now I must insist that you go inside and wait for me there! When I return, I and I alone shall decide what is to be done with that wretched housekeeper! Do you understand me?"

"Yes," she said meekly, as she began to realize that she had no real grounds for complaint. "I only wanted to help, that's all. I understand that you're upset, and that what happened to poor Catherine was utterly horrifying, but nothing can be done for her mortal body now. There is only her spirit to consider, and I think it would be more sensible to take some time trying to determine what she actually wants."

She waited, but he failed to reply. Not knowing whether he'd heard her or not, she tried to think of some way she might be able to get through to him, before reminding herself that she had to learn her place. As much as she wanted to talk Richard out of this madness, she could only watch for a few seconds as he threw the shovel aside and reached his hands down into the mud. Finally, supposing that he would eventually calm down once he was back in the house, she turned to walk away.

"She is gone," he said suddenly.

Stopping, she looked back and saw him kneeling in the mud. Confused, she walked over and looked down to see that he was holding what appeared to be an empty cloth sack. Rain was still falling, washing mud from the sack, but Rebecca could already see that there was no sign of a body. A moment later Richard set the empty sack aside and reached his hands into the mud, searching for any hint of Catherine's corpse while muttering madly to himself under his breath.

Rebecca could only watch this hopeless operation, and after a few seconds she saw that one end of the supposed grave was dominated by thick, bulging roots from the oak tree. She still wanted to find some way to help her husband, and finally he leaned back with his hands still in the mud and let out a heavy sigh. Rebecca watched the side of his face and tried to imagine the pain he was feeling; although Richard had barely spoken about Catherine, he was clearly horrified by her fate.

"She is gone," he said again.

"Perhaps she is deeper still," she suggested.

"I do not believe that is possible."

"Then perhaps nature has taken its course. I do not know how long it takes for the worms to..."

Her voice faded as she realized that she should perhaps not speak to openly about the possibility of Catherine's body being consumed by all the creatures in the soil. Besides, even with her limited knowledge of such things Rebecca felt fairly sure that there should at least be some bones left.

"Then what has happened?" she asked finally.

Taking the sack again, Richard got to his

feet and turned to her.

"That woman must have lied again," he said after a moment. "It's the only possible explanation."

"Might Catherine not have found some way to climb out of her grave?" she asked. "What if she escaped and somehow made a bid for freedom?"

"She would have had scant minutes in which to do so," he pointed out, "and I'm sure that both Fanny and Oliver would have still been here when she escaped."

"Then she *must* be down there," she said, looking once again at the mud.

"She is not. Her grave is empty." He looked down at the sack in his hands, as if he was lost in thought. "And if her grave is empty, that can only mean that she was never put here. I fear that Mrs. Baxter spun another false tale, perhaps in an attempt to fool me. Even now, she seems to not want to be honest about what really happened on that awful day."

"Then what do you think happened?" she asked.

"I do not know," he replied, before stepping past her and heading through the rain, making his way toward the house, "but this time, I am going to uncover the truth."

AMY CROSS

CHAPTER TWENTY-ONE

"SHE WATCHES," FANNY MUTTERED, while tapping her left foot frantically against the floor, "and she waits. But why? If she means to take her revenge, then why does she not just take it now?"

Turning to look at the doorway, she once again saw Catherine's shadowy figure in the darkness.

"I'm right here!" she screamed, getting to her feet. "I'm here, Catherine! What do you want from me? You've already killed my husband, so why not take me next?"

"Do you still say that she is not as mad as a dog?" Richard asked Rebecca. "I daresay she no longer even remembers the truth, in which case she is no use to any man." Reaching past his wife, he once again picked up the pistol. "She will tell me what truly happened, or in the name of the Lord I shall end her miserable suffering forever."

"Richard -"

"I have listened to you up until this point," he continued, cutting her off, "but no more. This is my house, Rebecca, and I would remind you that ultimately the decisions are mine to make. I understand that you might not want to see this, in which case you are free to excuse yourself. In fact, I think it would be better if you did just that. What happens next to Fanny might not be suitable for your eyes."

"You -"

"Who goes there?" he shouted suddenly, pushing past Rebecca and aiming his pistol out into the hallway. "Speak now or I shall not be responsible for what happens next!"

"Did you see someone?" Rebecca asked.

"It's her," Fanny said from the chair. "She plays with us, as a cat plays with a mouse."

"I will not suffer intruders in my own home," Richard snarled, taking one of the candles and hurrying into the hallway, then aiming the pistol all around. "You would do to come out and explain yourself," he continued, "else I shall be entirely within my rights to blast your head clean open. If you believe me to be a liar, then I dare you to come at me and find out the truth for yourself."

"She's taking her time because she knows

she has all night," Fanny sobbed.

"Where is her body?" Rebecca asked, hurrying to the chair and dropping to her knees, then looking up into Fanny's eyes. "I heard what you claimed earlier, but Richard is sure that there is no body in that grave. Is there any chance that you might have forgotten part of the story?"

"I buried her myself," she replied, as Richard continued to shout warnings in the hallway. "We waited a while after the deed was done. There is no-one who could possibly have survived such a fate."

"Then where *is* she?" Rebecca hissed. "None of this makes any sense!"

"She's here," Fanny told her. "That's all that matters now. She's here and she intends to make me pay for what happened, and likely she'll want her revenge upon you as well."

"Me?" Rebecca asked. "What did I do to her?"

"You took her husband," Fanny said with a faint smile. "Oh, you sweet young thing, you do not understand the ways of the heart, not so very much. Catherine will see you as an interloper, as one who took her place in this mortal world. She will not stand to see you with Richard for much longer. Mark my words, once she has taken me, you will be next!"

Before she could answer, Rebecca heard

Richard storming back through and she turned just in time to see his slam the door shut. She opened her mouth to ask him what he was doing, but he immediately grabbed the nearest table and pulled it into place so that it was blocking the door from opening. Stepping back, with the pistol still in his right hand, he seemed utterly horrified.

"Someone has come for me," he stammered breathlessly. "I can only assume that it must be some enemy of my family."

"Enemy of your family?" Rebecca replied. "Why would -"

"The Hadlows are hated by many," he continued. "I'm sorry, I did my best to hide the truth from you." He turned to her. "During the days of the last king, my father and his brothers picked the wrong side. They were guided by their faith, they believed that King James must be allowed to take his rightful place upon the throne, and that it was almost heresy to bring the hated Dutchman over instead. My father laid down his life fighting for what he thought was right, and then his cause was utterly destroyed. The Hadlows are now looked upon as traitors, almost, even though I am the only one left and I was never part of my father's group. I chose to stay out of the broader politics, in the hope that I would be spared retribution, yet now someone has seen fit to come and finish me off."

"It's not what you speak of," Fanny told

him. "Catherine -"

"One more word!" he roared, turning and aiming the pistol directly at her face. "Speak one more word of Catherine, you wretched old crone, and I shall discharge this in your face!"

Fanny stared at him for a few seconds, before starting to laugh. Rocking back and forward, she seemed to have completely lost her mind, and a moment later she let the metal crucifix fall to the floor.

"This country will never be strong again," Richard continued, "so long as it is turned against itself. Why can other men not see that?"

"Did you see who's out there?" Rebecca asked, as she began to wonder whether her husband might be correct.

"Mere shadows," he explained. "Slips in the darkness. Evidently this fool means to torment me before he makes his move. As far as I can make out, there might be just one of them. But by entering my home unbidden, this miscreant has invited death upon himself."

"I thought it looked like a -"

Rebecca stopped herself just in time. She had been about to tell Richard that the intruder had – at least from her limited vantage point – appeared to be a woman, but she knew that she should better hold her tongue. Instead, hearing more laughter, she turned and saw that Fanny appeared now to be a woman entirely broken, rocking frantically in the chair as if greatly amused by some voice or thought that only she could hear.

"Her mind is gone," Rebecca whispered. "The poor woman. She -"

Suddenly spotting movement nearby, she spun around. Letting out a gasp, she fully expected to see someone in the far corner of the room, yet now the shadows had returned to normal. A moment later, however, she heard footsteps crossing the room, as if some invisible figure had most certainly broken through the barricaded door. Turning to Richard, she saw the fear in his eyes and realized that he too was aware of the presence.

"The cut on my cheek," she said, her voice tense with fear, "I must confess was caused by something I do not understand."

"Where is he?" Richard snarled through gritted teeth. "I will have his head!"

He aimed the pistol toward the far end of the room, as if he expected his foe to appear at any moment. Rebecca realized after a few seconds that she had begun to hold her breath; she took a step back, watching the shadows, and now she felt more certain than ever that she was being watched. She wanted to warn Richard, yet she knew that he would quickly dismiss such a foolish notion. As Fanny continued to laugh childishly in the chair, Rebecca took a few more steps back until she bumped against the dresser next to the older woman, and then she waited as her heart pounded in her chest.

And then, as she looked over at Richard again, she spotted a woman's face reflected in the window.

"Richard!" she shouted, pointing at the window. "There!"

Turning, Richard immediately fired his pistol, shattering the glass. Wind and rain began to blow into the study, but there was once again no sign of an intruder. Rebecca tried to work out where the woman must have been standing for her face to appear like that in the darkened window, and after a moment she turned to her husband.

"Richard," she said, watching as he began to reload the pistol, "I have never seen a portrait of poor Catherine, do you have -"

Before she could finish, she saw to her horror that the dead woman was standing directly behind him. She stared for a moment, unable to comprehend what she was witnessing, but after a few seconds she realized that Richard was oblivious as Catherine reached up to put a hand on his shoulder.

"No!" Rebecca blurted out, before grabbing the metal crucifix from the floor and holding it up, rushing forward toward Catherine.

In that instant Catherine's ghost screamed and vanished into thin air. Shocked, Richard spun round to look just as Rebecca stopped next to him with the crucifix still raised in her hand.

"I told you," Fanny chuckled from the chair, "she can't be stopped. "She *will* take her revenge."

"I heard that scream once before," Richard stammered, his face wracked by fear as he dropped the pistol onto the table and stumbled back, before slumping into one of the other chairs. "It was her. I swear I recognized it, I swear that was Catherine but..."

He turned to Rebecca.

"How is such a thing possible?" he continued, and now his voice was trembling with fear. "I saw her. I heard her, but I also know that she was buried in her grave. Where is her body?"

Rebecca opened her mouth to reply, but at the last moment she looked down again at the metal crucifix in her hand. Her mind was racing as she tried to determine exactly what was happening, and yet – despite the same gnawing headache that had been troubling her for a while now – she was starting to formulate an idea. She thought back to the seemingly empty grave outside, and to the sack from which Catherine's body had seemingly disappeared, and to the knotted roots of the dying old oak tree. The crucifix seemed to have at least some limited power to chase away Catherine's ghost, but this could not be relied upon forever. Finally, stepping forward, she placed the crucifix in

Richard's hands and squeezed his fingers tight around the metal.

"Keep hold of this," she told him, as wind continued to howl through the broken window. "You might need it, if indeed the ghostly presence is more angry at you and Mrs. Baxter than she is at me. And I..."

She paused as she realized exactly what she was going to have to do in order to prove or disprove her plan.

"And I," she continued, with a shudder passing through her chest, "have need of an oil lamp I can use in the rain."

AMY CROSS

CHAPTER TWENTY-TWO

PUSHING HER WAY THROUGH the terrible weather, Rebecca held up the brass lantern she had found in the dining room and prayed that it would last for at least a few minutes longer.

She almost slipped in the mud, but finally she reached the grave that Richard had dug up. The torn sack had been left on the ground, but it was not this that caught Rebecca's attention. Instead, as she set the lantern down under as much cover as she could manage, she took the shovel and began to dig down into the grave again, hauling as much mud out as possible as she tried to uncover the tree's roots. Sure enough, after a few minutes she was able to see a thick, knotted mass of old roots, and after setting the shovel aside she began to kneel in the mud so that she could see more clearly.

The roots themselves were huge, in some cases as thick and wide as a man's arm, and some of them wound round one another in ways that left large gaps. Rebecca knew very little of oak trees, still less of roots, and even less than that about the capacity of humans to survive in tight spots. However, as she used her hands to pull more mud away, she found several more gaps in the root system, and finally she found one particular gap that she felt sure was large enough to fit a human being.

She peered into the gap, but all she saw was darkness.

Opening her mouth, she considered calling out, but she knew deep down that there was nobody around to hear her words. Nevertheless, she knew that if she merely turned around now and returned to the house, she would feel as if she had failed, so she told herself that she had to prove to herself that there was no cause for concern.

Grabbing the lantern, she moved it closer and experimented with the angle until some of the flickering light penetrated the chamber inside the network of roots. A sharp pain was pounding at the back of her head now, seemingly tapping at the inside of her skull, but she knew that she had to stay focused. She tilted the lantern as much as she dared, but she still found that she was unable to properly see through into the dark space between the roots. Finally, placing the lantern down again, she took the shovel and began to chip away at the gnarliest of the roots, hoping to make an even larger gap while trying to avoid causing too much damage.

"I'm sorry," she said, briefly glancing up and seeing the oak tree rising high above her in the stormy weather. "I hope you can forgive me, but I must be sure."

She looked at the roots again, and for the next few minutes she could only bash away at the roots, breaking small sections off thanks to slow and somewhat torturous progress. Her arms were aching and she felt as if she was making a fool of herself, yet deep down she knew that there had to be a reason why Catherine's body had been missing from the sack, possibly a reason that would not have involved the poor woman hauling herself out of her own grave and then disappearing into the night.

Suddenly a larger chunk of the roots fell away, and Rebecca took the lantern again. She still had to experiment to find the best way of casting the light, but finally she was just about able to see into what appeared to be a fairly large open space that had been left between different sections of twisting root material. At first she was unable to really understand what she was seeing, but at the last moment – as she was about to pull back and try to come up with another idea – she spotted something that awfully like the bones of a human hand.

She froze, staring at the bones, which

appeared to be locked into a slightly curled formation. She told herself that she might be wrong, but then she tilted the lantern a little and saw what looked like the bone of a human forearm.

"Catherine," she whispered.

Leaning closer, she peered more deeply into the small chamber, and finally she let out a shocked gasp as she saw the true extent of the horror. Just as she had feared, Catherine had somehow made her way into this space deep beneath the tree, and her skeletal remains sat hunched in the hollowed nook. At least, Rebecca had to assume that this was Catherine; although the skull had little skin left to be picked away, there were some strands of fair hair still clinging to the bone, and the jaw had been left partially open as if the woman had died while either crying or screaming.

Looking up, Rebecca saw that some of the roots higher up bore evidence of thick scratches, as if Catherine had tried desperately to claw her way out from the chamber.

She returned her attention to the corpse, and she felt a shudder in her chest as she tried to imagine the woman's fear in her dying moments. Trapped all alone in darkness, deep beneath the surface and surrounded by only dirt and the roots of the tree, she must have quickly realized that her escape from the grave had granted only a temporary reprieve. How long her death had taken, Rebecca could not imagine, although she hoped that the end had been as speedy and as painless as possible.

"You poor thing," she said, reaching into the gap and touching one of the leg bones, which now had some kind of weed growing around its width. "You escaped from your grave, only to wind up in a different trap. And you have been here ever since."

Realizing that there was little she could do to help right now, she pulled her hand back and tried to work out how best to proceed. She would have to inform Richard of her discovery, of course, and she reasoned that he would then have to rapidly arrange for the body to be transferred to a proper cemetery. As far as she could imagine, Catherine must be desperate to have a proper burial, and Rebecca told herself that this must be the only sure way to end her anger forever.

Turning, she used the shovel for support as she hauled herself up, and then she began to climb out of the grave – only to freeze as soon as she heard a deep splitting sound coming from somewhere over her shoulder.

She looked back at the gap in the roots. She was holding the lantern now, but its flickering light no longer penetrated the dark little chamber beneath the tree. The splitting sound continued, however, and slowly twisted as if something inside the chamber itself was breaking. Rebecca looked up, worried that the root system was damaged and that the entire tree might topple over onto her, but a moment later she looked back into the darkness of the roots themselves; the splitting sound continued, but it was a frantic, inconsistent sound that seemed to ebb and flow with varying degrees of strain.

Rebecca opened her mouth to call out, but she found that she dared not speak.

Instead, slowly, she stepped back to the other end of the grave and crouched down. Staring into the dark gap, she told herself – as the splitting and ripping continued – that she merely had to illuminate the gap and prove to herself that the sound was normal. She still hesitated, however, as she felt fear tightening in her chest, and she began to wonder whether she might instead retreat and fetch her husband so that he could deal with the problem.

After all, was that not what husbands were for?

She lingered, however, and after a few seconds she began to lean forward. Although she felt terribly afraid, she also believed that even a woman should be able to show bravery once in a while. She held the lantern up so that its glow once again penetrated the chamber, and then – as rain continued to fall – she allowed herself a sigh of relief as she saw that the corpse of Catherine Hadlow had not moved at all.

Drops of rain were falling all around the

entrance to the chamber, and a few drops were even falling inside as well, but the strange splitting sound had inexplicably stopped.

"Well," Rebecca whispered, feeling a little foolish now for having expected anything else, "I suppose we had all better be -"

Suddenly the corpse's head turned, until its rotten face was staring straight at her.

Rebecca opened her mouth to cry out, but at that moment the dead woman lunged at her, reaching out with a rotten hand and grabbing her by the throat.

CHAPTER TWENTY-THREE

PULLING BACK, REBECCA FELL away from the
dead hand and landed with a thud in the dirt. The
lantern landed next to her and tilted onto its side,
with the glass breaking and the light quickly
fizzling to nothing.

In the darkness, with almost no moonlight at
all, Rebecca could just about see Catherine
Hadlow's rotten corpse reaching out from the hole,
trying to grab her. Something seemed to be holding
Catherine back, however, and after a few seconds
Rebecca realized that roots and vines had grown
into and through the dead woman's bones,
functioning like strings that held her back.
Catherine snarled and tried again to lunge forward,
ripping and splitting some of the threads but only
managing to break a little further out of the

darkness. Snarling again, the dead woman pulled harder, this time causing a slow cracking sound to ring out.

"I'm sorry," Rebecca stammered, filled with panic as she turned and tried to climb out of the muddy grave, "I must fetch -"

In that instant, she slipped in the mud and crashed back down to the bottom, landing in a soaked pile. She began to sit up, only to feel a gnarled hand grabbing her left ankle; turning, she saw that Catherine was slowly but surely tearing herself free from the roots and vines that were holding her back. Clearly furious at her restraints, Catherine twisted and wriggled, slowly clawing her way out from her resting place, and a moment later she managed to lunge forward again.

Scrambling back to the grave's other end, Rebecca grabbed the shovel and threw it helplessly toward the dead woman. The shovel missed and Catherine snarled again, and this time – as she pulled forward once more – she managed to tear away from one of the larger vines that had been running through her chest. Almost halfway out of the chamber now, she reached for Rebecca's leg, furiously snatching at her as her angry growl continued.

Realizing that she had to get to safety, Rebecca once again tried to climb out of the grave. This time she was more careful, making sure not to slip, and after almost a full minute she managed to roll over the grave's top and out onto the ground. Rain was still pounding down, and cold mud was soaking through her clothes, but Rebecca could see the house now and she knew that she simply had to tell Richard what she'd found. She got onto all fours, ready to clamber to her feet, yet after a moment she hesitated as she felt a faint twisting pain growing ever more intense in the back of her head.

Wincing, she tried again to stand, but instead she found herself staring down with a sense of wonder at the mud. Her mind was screaming at her to get to the house, yet somehow some other impulse held her in place. Finally, forcing herself to be smarter, she stumbled to her feet and took a few paces forward, before stopping as she once again felt drawn to stay outside.

"Help me," she groaned. "Somebody, please, I think something's really wrong with me but I don't know what. I think I need..."

Her voice trailed off for a moment. She felt burning hunger in her belly now, the same hunger that had previously compelled her to feast on Oliver's dead body, yet now the sensation was much stronger and she realized that the body of one dead man would never be enough.

"I need..."

She hesitated as she felt herself becoming

increasingly weak.

"Richard, where are you? Richard, please, I'm scared..."

After a moment, for no reason that she could comprehend, she opened her mouth and stuck her tongue out. She felt a shiver of pleasure run through her body as she felt raindrops falling on her tongue, although this pleasure was tempered by the sudden sense that the water falling from the heavens was still somehow too clean and too pure.

As a shudder ran through her chest, she slowly turned in the rain as muddy water ran from her face. In that moment she found herself face-to-face with the dead body of Catherine Hadlow, who had followed her out of the grave and was now standing just a few feet away.

Rebecca opened her mouth to cry out, but some strange impulse was still keeping her quiet. She tilted her head slightly, staring at the dead woman's face, but after a couple of seconds she instead turned to look past Catherine. Staring into the rainy darkness, she realized that the dirty little river ran past the garden just a short distance away, and she found herself thinking of the thick, muddy, dirty water. A twist of pain rippled in her belly, reminding her of the glorious sensation of biting into Oliver Baxter's severed arm, but she quickly realized that she could probably find a fresher feast elsewhere.

"I'm sorry," she murmured, barely able to get the words out at all. "I'm... so sorry..."

Hearing a faint groan, she turned once again to Catherine. Although she knew she should scream and run, Rebecca instead found herself noticing the scraps of meat and tendons and flesh that clung to the dead woman's body and still somehow held her together. The sight was astonishing, yet Rebecca found herself wondering how this reanimated corpse might taste. After a moment, unable to help herself, she began to slowly reach out toward a dangling thread of meat hanging from Catherine's left arm. Taking hold of the meat, she tried to pull it away, only to find that it was attached to the bone.

After tugging a couple more times, Rebecca stepped forward, only to slip and fall down into the mud. Landing on her hands and knees, she began to retch slightly, but she found that nothing was coming up from the back of her throat. Instead, she quickly started looking through the darkness, and finally she crawled forward through the mud, heading in the general direction of the river.

"Richard," she whispered, struggling to even think as she a burning sense of hunger filling her belly. "Help me, I don't know... I don't understand..."

She began to crawl faster, even though she still didn't understand what she was hurrying toward. She felt increasingly determined to get to the river, and after a few more seconds she reached the edge of the riverbank and tried to crawl down. Instead she began to lose her balance, and she quickly tumbled down until she slammed against a bush and let out a cry of pain.

Shivering with pain and hunger now, she somehow managed to sit up. Her cold, wet clothes were clinging to her skin now, and she knew that she risked getting ill if she stayed outside for too much longer. Nevertheless, she could just about see rain peppering the river's surface, and she couldn't help thinking about all the rich water that was waiting for her.

"Richard, I'm sorry," she murmured, even though she knew he couldn't hear her at all. "I don't know what's happening to me, but I can't stop myself."

Scrambling down through the mud, she finally reached the water and plunged in, immediately crashing beneath the surface. After a few seconds she came back up, gasping for air in the darkness, and then she reached her hands out and felt the freezing, dirty water all around. Part of her mind was still telling her that she had to get back to the house, yet this part was becoming less and less prominent, fading toward the back of her mind while screaming in an attempt to remain strong. Finally there was almost nothing left of her former mind at all, and she merely stood waist-deep in the water and smiled, tilting her head a little as she realized that she finally felt as if she was home.

Her mouth slipped open, and after a couple of seconds she let out a faint, incoherent string of sounds that rolled together to form muted dirge.

Slowly she began to wade forward, making her way deeper into the river until only her head was still visible above the surface. She turned and looked all around, and her smile grew even wider as she saw all the foliage and detritus that had been left in the dirty water. She held her hands out further and felt scraps of material floating nearby, and as she took a deep breath her nostrils were filled with a foul, almost sulfur-like scent. She leaned her head back for a few seconds, enjoying the sense of being back where she belonged, and after opening her eyes she failed even to blink as raindrops fell against her pupils.

After managing to let out a few more unintelligible groans, she began to kneel in the river, slowly disappearing beneath the surface and sinking down into the cold, dark, dirty depths.

AMY CROSS

CHAPTER TWENTY-FOUR

"WHERE IS REBECCA?" RICHARD whispered darkly as he stood at an unbroken section of the window, staring out into the storm-ravaged night. "I should never have let her go out there alone. What kind of husband am I?"

"A dead one," Fanny replied.

He turned to her.

"Soon, anyway," she continued with a leering, delirious grin. "You *do* know that, Mr. Hadlow, don't you? When it comes to the living and the dead, the living don't have a chance. We know only this world, whereas the dead... the dead know both, and they have brought back with them dark arts from beyond the veil."

"I should have put you down like a dog already," he murmured. "It would have been preferable to letting you live this long."

"Oh, please do so," Fanny said, slowly lifting herself up from the chair on weak, tottering legs. "Mr. Hadlow, I saw the fear in my dead husband's eyes and I do not want to suffer the same fate. You have a fine flintlock pistol there, one I believe that belonged to your father, so why not use it? You would be hastening my departure to Hell, but at least you would be shortening my suffering in this world."

"Why did you do it?" he asked. "Why did you bury poor Catherine alive?"

Smiling again, Fanny reached out and steadied herself for a moment against the table.

"For you," she purred finally.

"Errant nonsense!"

"You would prefer to have a crippled wife?" she asked. "One who could not possibly give you children?"

"I would prefer that you had not done such a wicked thing to the woman I loved!"

"But you love Rebecca too," she pointed out. "You don't love each woman individually, Mr. Hadlow, so much as you love the idea of a wife. The idea of children. The idea of the perfect home. The idea that your family's name can be salvaged after all the wrongs committed by your father and your uncles."

"You don't know what you're saying," he

sneered.

"Oh, but I do," she said, taking a limping step forward. "Do you remember all the times I reassured you, Mr. Baxter? Do you remember all the times I told you that your family's name would recover and that this house would be your salvation?" She paused, staring at him with a growing sense of contempt. "All lies," she sneered. "I told you what you wanted to hear, but in truth this house was an abomination and a mistake from the start. Why, I am sure that its very bricks are imbued with the pain and desperation that constitutes your pathetic so-called family."

"You would be wise to remember your station," he said through gritted teeth, as he adjusted his grip on the pistol. "A crazed dog that barks at its owner is not long for this world."

"And I have already told you to do it," she reminded him. "I *want* you to put me to death, so why not hasten the moment by being honest with you? The Hadlow family name can never recover from your father's actions, Sir. You might as well give up. This pathetic house just makes you look like a bigger fool than ever. Would you really want to bring children into this world who must share the same burden of shame that drags you down? What miserable -"

"Stop!" he roared, raising the pistol and aiming it straight into her face.

"Do it," she replied. "Save me from -"

She stopped as they both heard a heavy thud coming from out in the hallway.

"But it is too late," Fanny said softly. "That much is certain now. Catherine's spirit might have failed to get us, but I fear her form itself has now risen from the ground. That will certainly be too much for either of us to handle." Reaching up, she grabbed his hand and tried to force him to pull the trigger. "Do it, Sir," she added, as fresh tears filled her eyes. "Save me from her!"

Richard struggled to keep the gun from firing, before pulling it away from her grasp.

"Coward!" she spat back at him. "You utter, ridiculous coward! Why can't you do this for me? Why must you leave me to -"

Before she could finish, a knock rang out. They both turned and looked over at the door, just as the first knock was followed by another, then another. The door was still shut, but now neither Richard or Fanny could fool themselves into believing that there was nobody on the other side. They both stood in complete silence for a moment, before Richard took a step forward.

"No!" Fanny hissed, grabbing his hand.

"It might be Rebecca."

"It's not Rebecca! It's Catherine!"

He turned to her.

"She means to do me harm," she sobbed,

before dropping to his knees, still clutching his hand and squeezing much tighter now. "Sir, she means to make me suffer something bad!" She tried to take the pistol from him. "Do me the good service of stopping that, Sir. Please, I beg you, let me be dispatched before she gets her hands on me, for I know that you at least will serve me my fate quickly, whereas she will take her time in tearing me apart!"

Barely even hearing the woman's words, Richard stared at the door with a growing sense of fear. A moment later he heard another knock, then two more, and a shiver rippled through his chest.

"I just want to die!" Fanny whimpered, clawing at his hand now, trying to make him use the pistol. "Oh Sir, I can't face her, not after what I did! I can't face the abomination of the dead!"

"Then you should not have earned her ire," he replied, still keeping his gaze fixed on the door.

"I'm begging you," she cried, leaving the pistol alone now and resorting to hugging his legs as tears streamed from her face. "Show me mercy, Mr. Hadlow!"

"Yet is she wrong to come after you, Fanny?"

"Sir..."

"You buried her alive, certain to cause her great suffering. For all your claims to have been trying to do something good, you condemned her to the most awful death possible, and no amount of warbling can excuse your actions. You and Oliver both turned a blind eye to something so awful, so heinous, that I can scarcely comprehend how -"

He flinched as he heard another knock.

Then another.

And a third.

"Has she not earned her moment of justice?" he asked. "Who am I to deny her? I loved her once. Indeed, I love Rebecca now, but I remember my love for Catherine. I remember its shape and feel, and I would grant her – if it be in my power to do so – her moment of resolution." He paused, before stepping toward the door, only for Fanny to hold tightly on his leg in an attempt to keep him back. "This thing seems unnatural," he continued, "but I believe there is naturalness in it, if only we seek to find it. There are many in the land of the living who would seek vengeance upon my family, Fanny, and in some ways that is simply the way of the world. Why should it not be so for the dead?"

"Don't let her in!" she screamed, still holding his leg tight. "Sir, I'm begging you!"

"Leave off me," he muttered, trying to kick her away. "I shall deliver you to her."

"You can't!" she cried. "I saw the horror in Oliver's eyes! You can't let the same thing happen to me!"

"I cannot stand in the way of what is right,"

he said, before looking down at her. "Fanny, you surprise me. I thought you would at least meet your fate with some honor."

"I -"

Before she could finish, he reached down and grabbed her by the shoulders. She struggled to twist free, but he quickly threw her back against the wall before turning and heading toward the door. Just as he reached for the handle, he hesitated as he heard another three knocks coming from the other side.

"Don't do this!" Fanny screamed.

"Dear Lord," Richard whispered, trying to find the remaining strength he needed, "grant that aside from my many errors as a man, I have always tried to do the right thing."

He held the handle for a moment, before turning it and slowly opening the door. And in that instant, finally, he found himself face-to-face with the rotten, standing corpse of the woman he had last seen as she lay impaled in the pit of the house's foundations.

"Catherine," he stammered, as Fanny screamed behind him and as tears flowed from his eyes. "Fanny Baxter is here. If you want her, she is yours."

CHAPTER TWENTY-FIVE

January 1689...

"MR. HADLOW CAN FIND another wife," Fanny told Oliver, as Catherine whimpered on the ground. "One who can give him a family. One who can make him happy. This one..." She looked down at Catherine's tear-filled eyes. "This one can do neither," she added. "Not now. Yet Mr. Hadlow is too good a man to make such a decision. So it must be made for him."

With that, she shoveled dirt onto Catherine's face, smothering the poor woman's cries even as she tried desperately to wriggle free from the sack. Turning, Catherine tried to find some way to crawl to safety; she reached out, but her hands felt only the thick roots of the oak tree as more and more dirt rained down upon her, crushing her beneath its increasing weight. She cried out again, screaming for help, begging Richard to appear and save her, but after a few seconds her cries turned to sobs as she realized that the weight of dirt was now almost stopping her from drawing breath.

She managed to pull her knees up and get onto her front, using her back to bear the weight while she desperately gasped for air. Wincing as the dirt tried to push her down, she reached again out through the top of the sack into which she had been placed; she felt the twisted roots, but a moment later her hand dipped into a gap. Instinctively she lunged forward, throwing herself into this gap and finding to her surprise that it seemed to have no limit. She grabbed the roots and pulled hard, wriggling out from the sack and squirreling her body from beneath the dirt. Clambering into darkness, she threw herself down and turned to look back as she heard the heavy, rhythmic thunder of her own grave being filled.

As she waited, she realized she could hear the sound of distant, muffled voices. She looked up, and to her surprise she spotted the tiniest gap of light somewhere above. Getting onto her knees, she leaned up closer to this gap; she could not see out, not properly, but now she was at least just about able to make out the voices a little more clearly.

"And good riddance to her," Fanny was saying, her voice thick with spite. "In truth, Oliver, I feel now that Mr. Hadlow should easily find himself a better wife."

"Do... do you think she is no more now?"

"She is buried," Fanny replied, as the regular shoveling thuds came to an end. "How long can she possibly hold her breath? If she is not dead already, she will be in a matter of seconds."

Catherine opened her mouth to call out, to tell them both that she had survived, but at the last second she held back. She had never liked Fanny Baxter, and she had always found the woman's husband Oliver to be a rather strange sort, and now she feared that they would do nothing to help her; indeed, she realized that they would only take further measures to end her life, so she held back as – a moment later – some shape briefly passed across the thin sliver of light. Holding her breath, she heard what sounded like a shovel being rested against the tree above.

"We will tell Mr. Hadlow nothing about this," Fanny continued. "We will tell him nothing that might slow his search for a new wife. That is understood, Oliver, is it not?"

"Yes, but -"

"Your first word there is correct, your second is not," she said firmly. "Oliver, we must make haste and find Mr. Baxter in Cobblefield, where he is surely trying to recover from today's horror. He might very well require our assistance. And then we shall never mention the wretched name of Catherine Hadlow ever again."

As she heard them walking away, Catherine made again to call for help; again, however, she realized at the very last second that to do so would only invite more injury. She waited as the tramping footsteps faded into the distance, and then she reached out and felt with her fingertips the knotted walls of her prison. She was deep in the root system of the old oak tree, in a small chamber that seemed by chance to have formed some distance beneath the soil. Telling herself that there must be some way out, she turned and tried to crawl away, only to immediately bump against another section of the root network. She fumbled, trying to work out which way to go, but in every direction her path was blocked by thick, twisted roots that were larger and stronger than any she had ever imagined.

She knew that there had to be some way out, yet so far she could find none. And all the while, the pain in her belly was getting worse and worse, and she began to feel hot blood leaking from the wound.

"Richard?" she stammered finally, even though she knew he was unlikely to be around. "Richard, can you hear me? I'm still alive, Richard. I'm not -"

Before she could finish, she felt something moving on her left arm. Instinctively pulling back, she froze in the darkness, but a moment later she felt the same sensation again, this time on one side of her face. She pulled away in the other direction, and then – looking up at the thin sliver of light – she spotted something small scurrying along one edge of a root section. Leaning up, she peered more closely, and she saw several ants scurrying down from the light to join her in the dark. Indeed, with each passing second at least twenty or thirty were joining the gathering, and moment later Catherine felt several of them falling onto her face.

"No!" she shouted, trying to brush all the ants away. "Leave me alone!"

As she reached down to her belly, she felt fresh blood on the front of her dress and her sense of panic immediately increased. She tried to get to her feet, only to slam her head against the roots above, and now she started reaching out and trying to break away sections of the chamber walls. Every time she pulled on one of the roots, however, she found that they were far too solid to even move, and she began to realize that she was trapped. She still tried to break free, yet she could already feel herself weakening and after a moment her knees slipped in some of the fresh blood that had leaked from her wound. Finally, filled with terror, she looked up against at the tiny gap as more ants flooded down into the chamber.

"Help me!" she shouted, supposing that even Fanny would be better than being left to bleed and starve to death. After all, she might yet be able to reason with the woman. "Mrs. Baxter! Mr. Baxter! I'm down here! Please, you have to come back!"

She pulled again on the roots, but they felt more solid than ever and she knew that she would be unable to tear her way to freedom.

"Mrs. Baxter?" she continued, and now she found that she could barely raise her voice above a whisper. "Please, I'm still alive down here, you have to come and get me out! Get -"

Suddenly she felt more ants around the base of her neck. Filled with panic, she started trying to brush them away, only to swiftly realize that there were in fact ants all over her body. No longer able to ignore the sensation of all those little legs walking across her body, she frantically tried to

228

wipe them away from every part of her skin, even as more of them arrived to outnumber her completely.

"Help me!" she screamed. "Somebody get me out of here!"

***

Two days later, Catherine's dead body lay curled in the chamber deep within the tree's roots. Thousands upon thousands of ants had found her now, and were swarming all over her corpse, tearing away tiny scraps of meat. Where gaps in her body had formed, ants scurried in and out of these holes, often going deep inside her bones to seek the freshest and most promising sources of food.

Her eyes and mouth were open. She had died screaming, but now the scream was silent and all that emerged from her mouth were lines of ants, carrying pieces of flesh and meat up toward the tiny gap in the roots above. Some of the ants had even begun to bite Catherine's eyeballs, tearing at the surface with their mandibles, breaking apart the surface and crawling deeper and deeper inside the eyes themselves. And all the while, more and more ants were arriving to join the feast, eventually covering Catherine's body in such numbers that barely any part of her face could still be seen.

Up on the forest floor, lines of ants scurried to and from a few small gaps at the base of the old oak tree.

CHAPTER TWENTY-SIX

Nine months later...

RICHARD STARED AT CATHERINE'S ravaged face for a moment, horrified by the sight of the damage done to her features, before slowly stepping aside and gesturing toward Fanny on the floor.

"I shall not stand in your way," he said, his voice trembling with fear. "If it is her that you want, then you must satisfy yourself. I know better than to argue with the dead. And then..."

He paused, looking down, unable to meet her gaze.

"And then," he whispered, lowering his voice, "you will leave. There will be nothing more for you to take from this world. You will be done here."

He waited, and a moment later Catherine stepped into the room. At the same time, Fanny crawled on all fours to the far corner, shivering with fear as she desperately tried to get as far as possible from the dead woman.

"Please," she sobbed, "have mercy on me. I have never willingly done wrong, I have always sought to make peace in the world, for myself and for others. I have always tried to do the right thing!"

"I will have no part of this," Richard said darkly as he watched Catherine stepping slowly toward Fanny. "You will do to her whatever must be done, and then that will be the end of the matter." He hesitated, watching as Fanny tried to hide behind the chair, and then he turned to leave the room. "Pray be done with her quickly, and do no more harm than -"

"Richard."

Stopping in the doorway, he realized that this voice belonged not to Fanny, but that instead Catherine had somehow managed to speak. He desperately wanted to hurry away, to avoid any further contact with the dead woman, but after a few seconds he turned; deep down, he was still hoping that his assessment might be wrong, yet he quickly found that Catherine had indeed turned her head so that she could look at him directly.

"Are you leaving?" she asked, as several ants crawled across the exposed bone and rotten flesh of her face. "Did you not miss me?"

"I -"

"Did you not mourn me?" she continued. "Your new wife is pretty, although I fear that all is not well with her. Do you know where she is now?"

"She.. went outside," Richard said cautiously. "Catherine, pray tell me, did you do anything to hurt her?"

"Not I," Catherine replied, and now her partially-skeletal features appeared almost to twitch in anticipation of a smile. "Not I, but another who perhaps was blind when he needed to see."

"I don't know what you mean," he told her. "Catherine, where is Rebecca?"

"She is outside," she replied, "though if you go to look, you might not see her. Perhaps you should have taken a little longer to find yourself a new wife, Richard. Was such haste really necessary? Could you not have waited even one year?"

"Catherine, what happened to you was not my fault."

"Yet you left me in the hands of those two butchers," she sneered, "and did not care to check that I was dead. You showed little respect for me as soon as you *thought* I was gone."

"Catherine, I only -"

Stopping suddenly, he realized that Fanny was no longer hiding in the corner. He looked around, expecting to find that she was hiding somewhere else in the room; she could not have slipped past him, yet there was no sign of her until he saw that the door to the storage room was now open. A moment later he heard a metallic clanking sound, and he realized that just a few seconds earlier a similar sound had caught his attention. And then, to his horror, he saw Fanny stepping back into view with an angry sneer on her face and Oliver's old long-handled ax in her hands.

"Fanny," he said, "what -"

"Die!" Fanny screamed, lunging at Catherine and swinging the ax wildly, hitting her in the shoulder and sending her thudding down to the ground. "Die again, you foul thing!"

Catherine tried to push her away, but Fanny kicked her hard in the chest, sending her crashing back down. Raising the ax up high, she quickly smashed it down, slicing through one side of Catherine's waist. Richard instinctively stepped forward to stop her, but at that moment Fanny swung the ax toward him, catching his left arm just below the shoulder. Feeling a burst of pain, he pulled back and bumped against the wall, and when he looked at his arm he saw that while the cut was not too deep, blood was soaking out onto his shirt.

"You shouldn't have interfered!" Fanny shouted at him, waving the ax around again. "None of you should have meddled!"

Behind her, Catherine was slowly standing again.

"To think that I tried to help you all," Fanny continued, stepping toward Richard and raising the ax again. "The Hadlow name belongs in the grave with the worms, and that's where I shall consign it tonight! There is no place for you in England now!"

She raised the ax high. Richard held up his hands as a form of defense, but at that moment Catherine lunged at Fanny from behind, placing her hands on the woman's face and immediately digging her thumbs into her eyes. Fanny screamed and tried to push her away, but she succeeded only in throwing the ax against the far wall as Catherine's rotten fingertips pierced her eyeballs.

Letting out a pained gasp, Fanny dropped to her knees. Blood was gushing from her eyes now and running down her face, but all Fanny could manage was a series of groans as she reached out with her hands and tried desperately to find the ax again.

"Sir!" she stammered. "I beg of you, end this pain one way or the other!"

Clutching his injured arm, Richard could only stare in horror as Catherine's fingers dug ever deeper into Fanny's eye sockets, gouging out what was now left of the orbs that had once occupied that space. Several ants were already scurrying off Catherine's hands and entering the sockets; some of these ants were immediately washed out by the flowing blood, but some disappeared into the sockets as Catherine finally began to retract her fingers to reveal the dark, ruined eyeballs within.

"Sir," Fanny whimpered, "let me go to my Oliver now."

"Do you know how it feels to starve to death?" Catherine sneered, reaching down and taking a firm hold of Fanny's jaw. "Do you know how it feels to waste away in agony?"

"Please," Fanny gasped, "I only meant to do the right thing! I never -"

"Enough with your lies!" Catherine snarled, before twisting her hands against Fanny's jaw. Seconds later the jawbone snapped, and Catherine twisted it the other way before pulling it off entirely. "Now you can never speak of such things ever again!"

Letting go of Fanny, Catherine watched as the dying woman slumped forward against the floor. Shuddering and spluttering, Fanny tried to crawl forward, only to immediately roll onto her side. Blood was pouring from what remained of her mouth, but when she tried to scream she succeeded only in spraying yet more blood across the floor. She reached out with her hands, trying to find something she could use to defend herself, and then she tried several times to get to her feet, each time with varying degrees of desperate failure.

"Let her live the rest of her miserable existence like this," Catherine sneered. "Let her know pain and suffering the way -"

Suddenly a shot rang out and Fanny's head exploded, splattering blood across the wall. Catherine turned and saw that Richard had drawn his pistol, and that he had ended Fanny's torment forever.

"This is no way for the just and the godly to behave," he said, staring at Fanny's corpse for a moment before lowering the pistol and turning to his dead wife. "You came for justice and you have it, and more besides. If I could change what happened and conspire to bring you back to this world, I would do so, but such matters are entirely out of my hands. I will endeavor to do whatever I can to give you a proper burial, Catherine, but you belong now in the world of the dead. I bid you farewell as you go to that place."

He waited, but she simply stared at him as if she failed to understand what she'd been told.

"I am done here," he added, turning and setting the pistol down. His hands were trembling and all he could think was that he wanted the night to be over. "Let the past remain the past now, for the world must move on."

He took a deep breath, but a moment later he felt Catherine's hands on the side of his face, holding his head tight as her fingertips moved toward the edges of his eyes.

"My darling," she sneered, as she leaned close to him from behind, "I am not finished with you yet!"

CHAPTER TWENTY-SEVEN

SUDDENLY BURSTING UP FROM beneath the river's murky surface, Rebecca gasped for air as she fell back against the muddy bank. Desperately trying to get air into her lungs, she lay bathed in a growing patch of moonlight, and after a few more seconds she began to bring up heavy gulps of foul water.

Rolling onto her side, she brought up as much of the water as possible, before scrambling onto all fours and crawling up the river's bank. Finally she throw herself onto the grass, digging her fingertips into the mud, and as she looked across the garden she saw the house standing dark and silent just a couple of hundred feet away.

"Richard," she spluttered, as she looked around and saw no sign of anyone else. Even the horrific, rotten form of Catherine Hadlow had disappeared. "Richard, where..."

She hesitated, and in that moment she heard the unmistakable sound of Richard Hadlow screaming in the house. Startled, Rebecca got to her feet; soaked from head to toe in the river's dirty water, she was shivering now in the cold night air, but Richard's cry continued for several more seconds before fading into a series of brief, guttural moans.

"Richard!" Rebecca shouted, pulling the hem of her soaked dress up as she began to run across the lawn, racing back toward the house. "Richard, what's happening! Richard, I'm coming!"

***

Stumbling into the darkened house, barely able to see a thing as she hurried across the hallway, Rebecca finally reached the door to the study.

"Richard!" she called out. "What -"

Stopping in her tracks, she saw Fanny's bloodied corpse on the floor with most of its head missing. A moment later, hearing Richard's gasps, she looked toward the far side of the room and saw to her horror that her husband was on his knees. The rotten corpse of Catherine Hadlow was standing behind him, slowly pressing her fingertips into his eyes as he tried in vain to pull away. Somehow she seemed able to keep him in place through sheer force of will alone, and after a moment Rebecca saw the first trickle of blood run from the corner of his right eye.

"No!" she shouted, racing forward and grabbing him, pulling him away from Catherine and then making sure to stand between the two of them. "Leave him alone!"

"I thought you'd drowned," Catherine replied. "You seemed so intent on throwing yourself into that river. Do you know why?"

"Get back" she stammered. Spotting the metal crucifix, she grabbed it and held it up, hoping that it would warn Catherine to stay away. "He didn't do anything to you!"

"He left me to die," she pointed out.

"He's a good man," she said firmly, through gritted teeth. "He doesn't deserve to suffer like this!"

"Do you love him?"

"I -"

Stopping suddenly, Rebecca realized that she wasn't sure how to answer that question. In truth, she barely knew Richard at all, and she also wasn't entirely sure how love felt; her father had insisted that Richard was a good man, certainly the best man she could ever expect to marry, and that the black mark against his name would be more than offset by the fact that he retained his family's wealth. After a difficult start she felt secure with Richard, and she wanted to become the perfect wife, but she had no idea whether any of those impulses actually constituted love.

"I did not love him," Catherine continued. "He came to my father and asked for my hand, and my father accepted. I can't imagine that things were very different for you."

"I don't know him!" Rebecca sobbed.

"And yet you stand here, defending him."

"He's a good man," she said again.

"How can you be sure of that?"

"I just know it in my heart," Rebecca continued. "I don't understand quite how, but he's a good man who just wants to build something here. He's built this house, and now he wants to create a family to live in it, and in order to do that he brought me here to live alongside him, and..." She paused for a moment as she tried to understand exactly how she felt. "And I'm proud to do that," she added, "because I believe that his intentions are pure, and because he has fought for the chance to start something new. That's what this house is. It's a beginning, and it's going to stand for a long time, it's going to stand here for many years after he and I are long gone. It'll stand after all the rumors and lies have faded as well. This house, Hadlow House, will always stand as a testament to something that Richard Hadlow keeps secure in his heart."

She paused, before swallowing hard as she finally knew exactly what she meant.

"Hope," she added finally.

"And do you believe," Catherine replied slowly, her voice creaking slightly as she struggled to speak at all, "that you are going to live long enough to see all of this come to pass?"

"That is in the hands of my maker," Rebecca told her, feeling a newfound strength that was quite alien, "but that is my desire, yes. To be his wife, and to grow to love him."

She turned and looked at Richard; blood ran from cuts on his face, but his eyes were intact as he stared back at her.

"Then who am I to stand in your way?" Catherine asked, taking a step forward. "You are blind to so much, but I shall not tell you all these things."

Rebecca turned to her again.

"You can discover them for yourself," Catherine continued, and once again she seemed to be on the verge of a smile, "and I wish you great luck in doing so, for you do not understand that your fate is already set, just as my own fate was set from the moment I fell from my horse."

She stepped closer to Rebecca, and reached out, placing a hand on the side of her face before running her fingertips around to the back of her head.

"Interesting," she purred. "I was right."

"What do you want?" Rebecca asked, too scared to push her away just yet.

"I want you to face the truth," Catherine told her, "but I think perhaps you will have to do that in your own time. Tell me, though. Do you know the greatest secret that religion hides from the world?"

"I..."

"No soul can be guaranteed safe passage from this world to the next," Catherine continued, tilting her head slightly as a smile spread across what remained of her lips. "Richard is going to learn that, but first you're going to learn that becoming a Hadlow wife is the most terrible of all fates. My dear, I look into your eyes and I see it already." Reaching forward, she took hold of the crucifix and pulled it gently from Rebecca's hands. "Why kill you, when instead I can leave you to suffer the worst fate of all? A fate even more agonizing than my own."

"Leave her alone!" Richard gasped.

"Oh, Richard," she purred, still keeping her eyes fixed on Rebecca, "didn't you learn yet? It is possible to be a good man – the best man, the greatest man – and still burn in Hell."

In that moment, she clutched the crucifix to her chest. Letting out a gasp of pain, she pressed the metal even harder against her body as it began to burn through what was left of her bones. Her hand slipped from the back of Rebecca's head and she stumbled back, and a moment later she dropped to her knees. Bending forward until she was on all fours, she kept the crucifix held tight against her rotten chest until her ribs shattered inward and the metal crashed into her body. Letting out a pained gasp, she managed to look up at Rebecca and scream one final time, before her body crumbled away and fell to the floor as dust.

Stepping back, Rebecca stared in horror at the spot where Catherine had been. Wincing, she reached up and touched the side of her face, and for a few seconds she still felt the dead woman's cold hand on her skin, before this sensation faded to nothing. And then, hearing a gasp, she turned to see Richard trying but failing to get to his feet.

"My darling!" she called out, hurrying across the room and leaning down to support him. "It's over! She's gone!"

"It's not over yet," he replied through gritted teeth, as he looked at the pile of ash on the floor, with a few chunks of bone still poking out from the remains. "Not until I've done the right thing by her!"

AMY CROSS

CHAPTER TWENTY-EIGHT

One week later...

"YOU ARE A GOOD man, Mr. Hadlow," Father Ward said as they stood in the cemetery behind St. Leonard's Church in Cobblefield. "Any souls buried here shall surely rest in eternal peace."

"This is my hope," Richard replied, staring intently at the name of Catherine Hadlow etched on the gravestone. "I had hoped to bury her on my own land, but... I see now that she should have been here all along."

"And your servants, too," Father Ward added, looking past him. "It is rare that a man provides so fully for the final resting place of such..."

He hesitated, as if he wasn't quite sure how

to complete that sentence.

"Well," he added awkwardly, "those of lower social standing are not always afforded such dignity in death."

"They were people too," Richard said, turning to look at the graves of Fanny and Oliver Baxter. "I confess that I do not entirely understand the ways of the world, but I feel there is a reason we bury the dead in such a way. There must be some satisfaction, some comfort that they receive in the next world that prevents them coming back to us here. At least, that is what I hope. Do you believe that there is any sense in my words, or do I sound like a rambling madman?"

"I think you are very wise," Father Ward told him, "and I know for a fact that St. Leonard's will put your kind donation to good use. I really must thank you again, Mr. Hadlow. Out here, so far from any large town, we are rather short of benefactors, although of course everyone gives as they can."

Richard turned and looked beyond the low cobbled wall, and for a moment he could only watch the thatched cottages of the little village and wonder about the lives of their inhabitants. A little further along the curved lane, he could just about see the village's one inn, *The Shoemaker*, and he told himself that most likely many of the villagers would be in that place whenever they had a spare moment. He briefly wondered whether he should go and visit the inn and perhaps learn a little of the local chatter, and then he remembered that he needed to get back to Rebecca. Besides, he was unable to shake the fear that most people would recoil from his presence once they knew his surname.

"I should be going," he told Father Ward. "Thank you again for providing the service today, even if I was the only one who attended. I'm afraid my wife is still a little weak."

"I hope to see you again soon."

"You will, most certainly." With that, Richard turned and began to walk away. "I shall bring Rebecca to one of your services soon, once she is better."

"I look forward to it," Father Ward replied. "Mr. Hadlow, you are a good man."

Stopping as he neared the gate at the top of the steps, Richard turned to him.

"Why did you say that?" he asked.

"I'm sorry?"

"That's three or four times today alone that you've called me a good man," Richard pointed out. "Is there some reason?"

"There is no reason at all, Sir," Father Ward replied, "other than the fact that it is plainly evident to me. You have provided well for these poor unfortunate souls who recently lost their lives.

Many men would not. And for that, Mr. Hadlow, I am quite sure that you have the Lord's eternal gratitude."

***

"It is possible to be a good man – the best man, the greatest man – and still burn in Hell."

As he finished putting the final bolt in place a few hours later, Richard could still hear Catherine's dying voice echoing in his thoughts. In truth, those particular words had never really left him over the previous week, and they had instead been echoing in his thoughts, constantly returning to the front of his mind even when he tried to focus on something else. He had told himself that eventually they would fade, yet every so often some other element – such as the priest's words – brought the phrase back.

"It is possible to be a good man – the best man, the greatest man – and still burn in Hell."

Forcing himself to stop worrying, he climbed down from the ladder and took a few steps back. A delivery that morning had brought the one final touch that he had long intended to make to the grounds, and he felt a flicker of pride as he saw the arched iron rail that ran over the top of the main gate. He'd thought long and hard about this arch, and for a while he'd felt that he needed to be modest, but now for the very first time he found himself hoping that he could move past the troubles of his family. He'd made a last-minute change with the ironmonger in the village, and the result of that change was now visible to anyone who came near the property.

"Hadlow House," he whispered, reading the name from the arch. "Yes, this is how it should be. A man should not have to hide away from the world, especially when he has done everything within his power to do things the proper way. One day, the name Hadlow will be spoken of fondly again, and I can only hope that I am alive when that day arrives."

Looking toward the house, he spotted a face at one of the windows. Rebecca was peering out at him; she had been behaving strangely for a while now, seemingly slipping into regular phases during which she seemed not to be quite herself, and what had started off as merely a case of apparent weakness now seemed a little more serious. She was often aloof and withdrawn, and sure enough a moment later she stepped out of view, disappearing into the darkness of the house's interior.

Richard allowed himself a faint, sad smile. He really had no idea what was truly wrong with Rebecca, but he felt sure that she would eventually feel better. Time, he had always believed, was the greatest healer of all.

To prove that point, he stepped through the gate and made his way over to the old oak tree. Now that Catherine had been properly buried, the tree appeared to have recovered much of its old health, and Richard had hopes that it would soon be back to its best. Somehow the tree had come – in his mind – to symbolize much that was good and important about Hadlow House. The importance of the place was based not just on the house itself, but also on the large walled garden that had been created. In this sense, Richard felt that he had finally achieved his goal.

He had created his own private paradise.

Reaching out he touched the bark of the tree. He knew very little of such things, of course, but he couldn't shake the feeling that the tree looked and felt so much healthier, as if was thriving in the environment that had been created. He couldn't help but push gently, admiring the tree's sturdiness, and it was at this moment that he realized he had created something that would – with any luck – long outlast his own life. Indeed, as he turned and looked all around, he thought of generations to come. There would be people – families, descendants of his own line with Rebecca – living at Hadlow House for many years. He tried to imagine what these people of the future would be like, and how the house might look one hundred years in the future, and then even further.

1798.

1898.

1998.

How might things change? He could only hope that there would be improvements, and that Hadlow House would forevermore be a happy corner of the world. He certainly felt that he had done all that he could manage in that regard, and that he could trust those who came next. For that eventually to come around, however, he would need children of his own, and he told himself that he would soon be able to start a family with Rebecca. Indeed, when he glanced at the house again, he saw her face once more staring out at him from the windows. He smiled at her, and although she immediately pulled back out of sight he knew that his happy life with her was just beginning. And soon Hadlow House would fill with the cries of happy children running around.

At that moment, Richard Hadlow felt absolutely certain that the worst of times were truly in the past, and that the future was filled with brightness.

As he continued to look around, he failed to notice the ground beneath his feet. Already, his boots were being investigated by several busy, industrious little ants.

AMY CROSS

CHAPTER TWENTY-NINE

AFTER PULLING BACK FROM the window, Rebecca froze in the gloom of the study and tried to think properly. She'd seen Richard a moment earlier, out there pacing around in the garden, but something about his stare had sent a ripple of fear through her chest. And yet...

And yet, she felt as if her own mind was drifting in and out of some waking sleep.

Turning, she shuffled across the study and out into the hallway. She knew she needed to find some way to make her thoughts latch onto something real, but instead she realized that she was almost drifting through the world. She stumbled past the foot of the stairs and entered the dining room, and then she stopped in her tracks as she felt her mind starting to fade again. No matter how hard she tried to think of the world, and of Richard, she wondered whether some other sense had begun to push her own thoughts aside.

Without even thinking, she walked over to the window and sat down. The frame of this particular window had been damaged by rainwater, which had leaked through a hole higher up. The wood remained a little moist and damaged, and after a few seconds Rebecca reached out and began to use her fingertips to pull flakes of this wood away. Soon she was holding in her hand several fairly sharp little piece, and as she stared at them she began to feel a rippling pain in her belly. She tried to push that pain away, but after a few seconds she instead lifted the flakes of wood up and sniffed them carefully.

Something about their wetness made her feel ravenously hungry.

"Why?" she whispered, briefly regaining control of her senses again. "What am I to -"

She stopped suddenly, and then she raised her hand to her lips and slipped the pieces of wood into her mouth. She began to chew, crushing the slivers and ignoring any pain whenever they cut into her gums. She enjoyed the slightly moldy taste, and the sense of so many tiny flecks all over her tongue, and then she swallowed. As soon as most of the wood had gone down her throat, she began to peel more away from the window's frame, and she could feel her hunger intensifying as she told herself that soon her belly would be full. She slipped more wood into her mouth and chewed, but then she turned and looked across the room as she realized that there was something else that might satisfy her urges more quickly.

Getting to her feet, she hurried through to the pantry, and then to the small storage room at the side of the house. She looked over her shoulder, just to make sure that she wasn't about to be interrupted by Richard, and then she rushed to the corner of the room and crouched down. After moving aside the pots and pans that she'd placed there earlier, she pulled aside a roll of fabric to reveal the rotten remains of Oliver Baxter's arm. She'd managed to conceal this arm from Richard, who believed that it had been buried with the dead man, whereas in fact Rebecca had gone to great lengths to keep it for herself.

Peering more closely, she saw maggots crawling through the graying flesh. Her first thought was to brush these maggots aside, but at the last moment she realized that here was really no point. She watched their little yellow-white bodies for a few seconds, mesmerized by the sight of them, and she realized that in some ways she was envious; they were able to go about their business without having to hide their intentions, while she had to constantly watch out in case Richard arrived.

Now, sure that she was alone, she leaned down and began to sniff the severed arm, and she found that different sections had vastly different aromas. She searched for a few minutes, trying to find the best possible spot, and then she leaned closer and – while holding the arm in place with her hands – she began to chew at the scraps of meat. She felt some of the maggots fall into her mouth, but this didn't stop her and soon she was half chewing and half sucking on the meat and bones.

"Rebecca?"

Suddenly hearing Richard's voice, she turned and glared toward the open door. She heard footsteps far off in the house, so she quickly covered the arm again and wiped her mouth before getting to her feet and hurrying first into the pantry and then out into the kitchen, where she found that Richard was examining some fruit.

"There you are," he said with a smile. "Will you be able to amuse yourself for a few hours? I'm afraid I must complete one of the larger jobs that Oliver never really started."

***

Several hours later, Richard hauled another thick patch of vegetation from the river and threw it up onto the grass. His back and arms were aching with the effort, but he knew that the job had to be completed and he certainly had no desire to wait until he might find another laborer.

Besides, he rather enjoyed doing the work himself. He looked over at the gate and saw, once again, the name Hadlow House in black metal letters, and he reasoned that if the house bore his own title than he should not be ashamed to get his hands dirty.

When he looked down at his hands, however, he saw a couple of thick maggots wriggling on his palms, and he quickly flicked them into the nearby mud.

"Are you busy?"

Startled, he looked up and saw Rebecca standing at the top of the muddy slope. Silhouetted against the gray sky, she was staring down at him with the same intensity that she'd exhibited much of the time since arriving at the house.

"I'm cleaning out the river," he announced proudly. "Or trying to, at least. I know this sort of work might seem to be beneath a man of my stature, but I have never been afraid to break a sweat. Obviously Oliver would have done this, had he survived, but -"

"Have you seen Oliver?"

"I beg your pardon?"

"Have you seen Oliver today?" she asked. "Or... have you seen Mrs. Baxter?"

"I'm not entirely sure what you mean," he

replied cautiously. "Mr. and Mrs. Baxter have been dead for some time now, for a little more than a week."

"Dead?" She furrowed her brow for a moment. "Of course. I'm sorry, you must forgive my moment of silliness. In truth, I've been feeling a little out of sorts lately."

"I can tell," he admitted. "Rebecca, as much as I enjoy your company, there is no need for you to be out here in the cold. Would you not prefer to wait inside the house? I saw that you made preparations for a meal earlier. Have you managed to get any further?"

"I... don't know," she murmured.

"I shall have to find a cook soon," he muttered with a sigh. "I simply have no choice. Tomorrow I shall venture into the village again and ask around. There must be someone there who can come and work for me. Would you like that, Rebecca? Would you like us to have some help around the house again?"

He waited for an answer, but now Rebecca seemed to have returned to one of her regular blank states. Sometimes he found her simply standing somewhere in the house or garden, staring into space as her mind had entirely emptied from her body; when he tried to wake her from these states, she often required several seconds before she could even pretend to act normally again. Although he had been telling himself that eventually she was bound to come around, and that she was merely struggling after the horrific events that had occurred a week earlier, Richard couldn't help but wonder whether something more serious might be wrong.

"Rebecca?" he said after a few more seconds. "Can you hear me?"

Turning to him, she blinked impassively, as if she didn't even recognize her own husband.

"Rebecca," he said again, "it's me. Are you sure you wouldn't like to see a doctor?"

"I'm quite alright," she replied uncertainly. "At least, I think I am." She paused, before smiling and shaking her head. "Yes, of course I'm alright, there's really no need to be concerned. My darling, I shall return to the kitchen and prepare you a rich and hearty meal. Just the sort of thing that you deserve."

Richard opened his mouth to call after her, but she was already heading back to the house and he realized after a moment that he should perhaps just continue to give her some space. Instead, he returned his attention to the river, and after a moment he spotted a dead crow on the muddy riverbank. Wading over to take a closer look, he peered at the creature and saw to his horror that it was infested by maggots that were rapidly eating away at what remained of its flesh.

CHAPTER THIRTY

"THAT'S ONE DAY DONE," Richard said several hours later, once the fading sun had forced him to end his work for the day. "The river is utterly filthy. I can only hope that it will recover eventually."

Stopping in the hallway, he realized that the house seemed strangely quiet. He had expected to hear the sound of Rebecca working in the kitchen, and to smell something cooking; instead there was only silence, and his wife had even failed to light any candles. Confused, Richard removed his gloves before looking through into the study, and then he tried the front room. He stopped for a moment, wondering whether Rebecca might be upstairs, and then he headed past the dining room and through into the kitchen.

"Rebecca -"

He stopped again as he realized that there was still no sign of her. He looked around, more puzzled than ever, but after a few seconds he heard a faint squelching sound coming from the pantry. He walked to the door, and then he made his way across the room and headed into the small storage room at the side.

"Rebecca," he continued, "what -"

As soon as he saw her, he froze. Rebecca was on her knees in the gloom, frantically chewing on some kind of meat. For a few seconds Richard was unable to quite make out what he was seeing, and then as his eyes adjusted to the poor light he realized that one end of this meat was still just about connected to a dangling human hand. In that instant, he finally understood that his wife was gnawing on the severed arm of Oliver Baxter.

Looking up at him with frantic eyes, Rebecca still had strands of meat in her teeth.

"What are you doing?" Richard stammered, before turning and hurrying out through the pantry and into the kitchen. Stopping, he tried to make sense of what he'd seen, but a moment later he spun around as he heard Rebecca's footsteps.

She hesitated in the doorway, staring at him with wild eyes.

"What were you doing just now?" Richard asked, as he saw flecks of meat on her chin. "Rebecca, for the love of all that's holy, why were you..."

His voice trailed off as he realized that something about her eyes was very wrong; she seemed almost ravenous, as if filled with hunger, and a moment later she approached him and put her hands on his shoulders. Leaning closer, she began to sniff the side of his face.

"Whatever has possessed you?" Richard gasped.

Her mouth opened and she let out a series of faint, indecipherable gurgles that certainly matched no language that Richard had ever heard.

"I will not tolerate this," he told her. "What -"

Suddenly she gasped, as if in pain, and reached up. He watched as she ran her fingers through her own hair, moving her hand slowly around to the back of her head. She furrowed her brow, clearly puzzled, and then she let out a faint groan.

"I..."

She managed only that one word before falling silent again.

"Rebecca," Richard continued, "you will tell me what is happening, or by the grace of God I shall tie you down until a doctor can be found to see you. What..."

Before he could finish, he realized that he could smell a foul, sweet scent. He had noticed this scent once or twice over the previous few days, but it had never been strong enough for him to mention. Now, however, Rebecca pulled her hand away from the back of her head, revealing that her fingers were covered by blood and what appeared to be some kind of pale pus.

"Rebecca," Richard said firmly, as his voice trembled with fear, "what is wrong with you?"

He waited for an answer, before stepping around her. Although his hands were shaking, he reached up and moved her hair aside, and finally he saw that the back of her head – which had been hidden by her hair – had been badly damaged. A thick, old-looking wound had left a hole in her skull; dried blood was caked all around this hole, and as Richard looked closer he saw what seemed to be fragments of damaged bone. And then, just as he was about to ask Rebecca what could possibly have caused such an injury, he realized that something was moving deep inside the wound itself.

He pulled her hair aside a little more, and now he saw several small maggots wriggling in the wound. As if that was not sufficiently horrific, a moment later he spotted something large and white glistening even deeper, and he found himself staring at one of the large, bulbous maggots that he had occasionally seen by the banks of the river. Hearing more gurgled whispers slipping from his wife's lips, Richard pulled back and looked into her eyes, and now he saw that her pupils were distended.

In that moment he remembered her clambering out of the river after the carriage had toppled over. At the time she'd touched the back of her head as if injured, but then she'd insisted that she was fine. Now, however, he realized that she must have suffered a grievous injury that had been festering and developing ever since.

Suddenly gasping, she lunged at him and bit the side of his neck. He quickly pushed her away, but he could see the greed and hunger in her eyes and a moment later she stepped toward him again.

"Stay away from me!" he shouted, hurrying across the kitchen and grabbing his pistol, then turning and aiming it at her face. "Woman, you will not come near me, else I must defend myself!"

Almost falling over, Rebecca stumbled toward him and reached out with her trembling right hand. She managed another faint gasp, and in that moment Richard realized that whatever was staring out at him through Rebecca's eyes, it was most certainly not his wife. Instead, she seemed almost to have been taken over entirely by the thick maggot that even now was buried deep inside her brain.

"No!" Richard shouted as she lunged at him, and he instinctively pulled the pistol's trigger.

One side of Rebecca's head exploded and she stumbled back, immediately falling to the floor. Horrified by what he'd seen, Richard hurriedly reloaded the pistol before stepping over to Rebecca again. Looking down at her, he was about raise the pistol one more time when he saw that a large section of her skull had been destroyed by the blast. Brain matter was seeping out and blood was spreading in a pool across the floor. A moment later, the large white maggot tumbled out and landed wriggling on the wooden boards, and Richard instinctively moved his foot and crushed the wretched creature beneath his heel.

Then, looking at Rebecca's remaining eye, he saw her blink.

"Thank you, my love," she gasped, before falling still.

"Rebecca?" he stammered, before dropping to his knees and putting his hands on her shoulders. "Rebecca, can you hear me? Rebecca, you can't leave! Do you understand? Rebecca, come back to me!"

***

"It is possible to be a good man – the best man, the greatest man – and still burn in Hell."

Catherine's words once again echoed through Richard's thoughts as he stumbled out of the house. The setting sun was low in the sky now, its light struggling to break through the tree of the forest. Richard took a few steps away from the house, before his knees buckled and he dropped down onto the ground. He stared ahead for a moment, but all he could see in his mind's eye was the sight of Rebecca's one remaining eye, filled with the most awful fear.

"Rebecca," he whispered, as a shudder passed through his body. "Please..."

He tried to think of the better times, of the moments when he'd felt close to Rebecca, but in truth the awful moment of her death seemed to have entirely erased any other memories. Even when he briefly managed to push the thought of her dying gasp aside, it was merely replaced by Catherine's haunting, mocking tone. And as tears run from his eyes and down his cheeks, Richard realized that ever since her fall into the river Rebecca must have been struggling to maintain her thoughts as that awful creature had burrowed deeper and deeper into her mind. Indeed, although he could scarcely comprehend the idea, he found himself wondering if the creature had begun to take her over entirely.

Now, as Catherine's words returned to him once more, Richard raised the pistol and placed one end on his mouth, while tightening his finger against the trigger.

"It is possible to be a good man – the best man, the greatest man – and still burn in -"

As soon as he pulled the trigger, Richard's head was blasted open. Nearby, birds immediately took off from the tops of the trees, taking flight high above as the dead man's corpse slumped down against the grass outside Hadlow House.

EPILOGUE

WITHIN MINUTES, THE SILENCE was broken as the birds returned.

Some sat on the treetops again, but others landed on the ground. Their black, beady eyes flicked constantly, but gradually some of the birds began to make their way across the garden, hopping closer to the bloodied corpse on the grass. One bird flew briefly before landing on the corpse's back, and then it began to peck at the meaty pulp at the top of Richard's neck. Other birds, meanwhile, were starting to approach some of the brain matter that had been blasted across the garden, and soon more and more of these birds found the courage to make their way closer to the corpse so that they could start feeding.

They weren't alone.

Soon the ants arrived, crawling onto Richard's hand and then along his arm before investigating his spilled blood and brain. They were joined by flies, and then by some of the birds that had flown from a little further away. A few hours later some rats emerged from the forest and scurried over to the body, and they began to tear at what was left of Richard's brain. As if word had somehow got out, all the creatures of the forest began to venture onto the garden, some of them passing through the open gate, moving beneath the arch as they approached the body and found a spot from which they could feed.

As the feast continued, the light eventually faded entirely. Hadlow House was now bare and empty and shrouded in darkness, and it stood in silence for several more hours until – just after three in the morning – one of the upstairs doors suddenly slammed shut.

1689

AMY CROSS

NEXT IN THIS SERIES

1722

(THE HAUNTING OF HADLOW HOUSE BOOK 2)

Hadlow House has stood empty ever since the tragic events that claimed the lives of its first owner. Now, however, a new family is moving to the house, bringing fresh life to halls and rooms that have for so long remained dormant.

But do echoes of the past remain, lurking in the shadows?

At first Hadlow House seems idyllic, but cracks soon start to show. Old voices are heard, but are they offering threats or a warning? By the time the truth becomes clear, Hadlow House might well be ready to claim yet another victim.

1722 is the second book in the *Haunting of Hadlow House* series, which tells the story of one haunted house over the centuries from its construction to the present day. All the lives, all the souls, all the tragedies... and all the ghosts. Readers are advised to start with the first book in the series.

AMY CROSS

Also by Amy Cross

The Haunting of Nelson Street
(The Ghosts of Crowford book 1)

Crowford, a sleepy coastal town in the south of England, might seem like an oasis of calm and tranquility. Beneath the surface, however, dark secrets are waiting to claim fresh victims, and ghostly figures plot revenge.

Having finally decided to leave the hustle of London, Daisy and Richard Johnson buy two houses on Nelson Street, a picturesque street in the center of Crowford. One house is perfect and ready to move into, while the other is a fire-ravaged wreck that needs a lot of work. They figure they have plenty of time to work on the damaged house while Daisy recovers from a traumatic event.

Soon, they discover that the two houses share a common link to the past. Something awful once happened on Nelson Street, something that shook the town to its core.

AMY CROSS

Also by Amy Cross

The Revenge of the Mercy Belle
(The Ghosts of Crowford book 2)

The year is 1950, and a great tragedy has struck the town of Crowford. Three local men have been killed in a storm, after their fishing boat the Mercy Belle sank. A mysterious fourth man, however, was rescue. Nobody knows who he is, or what he was doing on the Mercy Belle... and the man has lost his memory.

Five years later, messages from the dead warn of impending doom for Crowford. The ghosts of the Mercy Belle's crew demand revenge, and the whole town is being punished. The fourth man still has no memory of his previous existence, but he's married now and living under the named Edward Smith. As Crowford's suffering continues, the locals begin to turn against him.

What really happened on the night the Mercy Belle sank? Did the fourth man cause the tragedy? And will Crowford survive if this man is not sent to meet his fate?

Also by Amy Cross

The Devil, the Witch and the Whore (The Deal book 1)

"Leave the forest alone. Whatever's out there, just let it be. Don't make it angry."

When a horrific discovery is made at the edge of town, Sheriff James Kopperud realizes the answers he seeks might be waiting beyond in the vast forest. But everybody in the town of Deal knows that there's something out there in the forest, something that should never be disturbed. A deal was made long ago, a deal that was supposed to keep the town safe. And if he insists on investigating the murder of a local girl, James is going to have to break that deal and head out into the wilderness.

Meanwhile, James has no idea that his estranged daughter Ramsey has returned to town. Ramsey is running from something, and she thinks she can find safety in the vast tunnel system that runs beneath the forest. Before long, however, Ramsey finds herself coming face to face with creatures that hide in the shadows. One of these creatures is known as the devil, and another is known as the witch. They're both waiting for the whore to arrive, but for very different reasons. And soon Ramsey is offered a terrible deal, one that could save or destroy the entire town, and maybe even the world.

AMY CROSS

Also by Amy Cross

The Soul Auction

"I saw a woman on the beach. I watched her face a demon."

Thirty years after her mother's death, Alice Ashcroft is drawn back to the coastal English town of Curridge. Somebody in Curridge has been reviewing Alice's novels online, and in those reviews there have been tantalizing hints at a hidden truth. A truth that seems to be linked to her dead mother.

"Thirty years ago, there was a soul auction."

Once she reaches Curridge, Alice finds strange things happening all around her. Something attacks her car. A figure watches her on the beach at night. And when she tries to find the person who has been reviewing her books, she makes a horrific discovery.

What really happened to Alice's mother thirty years ago? Who was she talking to, just moments before dropping dead on the beach? What caused a huge rockfall that nearly tore a nearby cliff-face in half? And what sinister presence is lurking in the grounds of the local church?

Also by Amy Cross

Darper Danver: The Complete First Series

Five years ago, three friends went to a remote cabin in the woods and tried to contact the spirit of a long-dead soldier. They thought they could control whatever happened next. They were wrong...

Newly released from prison, Cassie Briggs returns to Fort Powell, determined to get her life back on track. Soon, however, she begins to suspect that an ancient evil still lurks in the nearby cabin. Was the mysterious Darper Danver really destroyed all those years ago, or does her spirit still linger, waiting for a chance to return?

As Cassie and her ex-boyfriend Fisher are finally forced to face the truth about what happened in the cabin, they realize that Darper isn't ready to let go of their lives just yet. Meanwhile, a vengeful woman plots revenge for her brother's murder, and a New York ghost writer arrives in town to uncover the truth. Before long, strange carvings begin to appear around town and blood starts to flow once again.

AMY CROSS

Also by Amy Cross

The Ghost of Molly Holt

"Molly Holt is dead. There's nothing to fear in this house."

When three teenagers set out to explore an abandoned house in the middle of a forest, they think they've found the location where the infamous Molly Holt video was filmed.

They've found much more than that...

Tim doesn't believe in ghosts, but he has a crush on a girl who does. That's why he ends up taking her out to the house, and it's also why he lets her take his only flashlight. But as they explore the house together, Tim and Becky start to realize that something else might be lurking in the shadows.

Something that, ten years ago, suffered unimaginable pain.

Something that won't rest until a terrible wrong has been put right.

Also by Amy Cross

American Coven

He kidnapped three women and held them in his basement. He thought they couldn't fight back. He was wrong...

Snatched from the street near her home, Holly Carter is taken to a rural house and thrown down into a stone basement. She meets two other women who have also been kidnapped, and soon Holly learns about the horrific rituals that take place in the house. Eventually, she's called upstairs to take her place in the ice bath.

As her nightmare continues, however, Holly learns about a mysterious power that exists in the basement, and which the three women might be able to harness. When they finally manage to get through the metal door, however, the women have no idea that their fight for freedom is going to stretch out for more than a decade, or that it will culminate in a final, devastating demonstration of their new-found powers.

Also by Amy Cross

The Ash House

Why would anyone ever return to a haunted house?

For Diane Mercer the answer is simple. She's dying of cancer, and she wants to know once and for all whether ghosts are real.

Heading home with her young son, Diane is determined to find out whether the stories are real. After all, everyone else claimed to see and hear strange things in the house over the years. Everyone except Diane had some kind of experience in the house, or in the little ash house in the yard.

As Diane explores the house where she grew up, however, her son is exploring the yard and the forest. And while his mother might be struggling to come to terms with her own impending death, Daniel Mercer is puzzled by fleeting appearances of a strange little girl who seems drawn to the ash house, and by strange, rasping coughs that he keeps hearing at night.

The Ash House is a horror novel about a woman who desperately wants to know what will happen to her when she dies, and about a boy who uncovers the shocking truth about a young girl's murder.

AMY CROSS

Also by Amy Cross

Haunted

Twenty years ago, the ghost of a dead little girl drove
Sheriff Michael Blaine to his death.

Now, that same ghost is coming for his daughter.

Returning to the small town where she grew up, Alex
Roberts is determined to live a normal, quiet life. For the
residents of Railham, however, she's an unwelcome
reminder of the town's darkest hour.

Twenty years ago, nine-year-old Mo Garvey was found
brutally murdered in a nearby forest. Everyone thinks
that Alex's father was responsible, but if the killer was
brought to justice, why is the ghost of Mo Garvey still
after revenge?

And how far will the real killer go to protect his secret,
when Alex starts getting closer to the truth?

Haunted is a horror novel about a woman who has to
face her past, about a town that would rather forget, and
about a little girl who refuses to let death stand in her
way.

AMY CROSS

Also by Amy Cross

The Curse of Wetherley House

"If you walk through that door, Evil Mary will get you."

When she agrees to visit a supposedly haunted house with an old friend, Rosie assumes she'll encounter nothing more scary than a few creaks and bumps in the night. Even the legend of Evil Mary doesn't put her off. After all, she knows ghosts aren't real. But when Mary makes her first appearance, Rosie realizes she might already be trapped.

For more than a century, Wetherley House has been cursed. A horrific encounter on a remote road in the late 1800's has already caused a chain of misery and pain for all those who live at the house. Wetherley House was abandoned long ago, after a terrible discovery in the basement, something has remained undetected within its room. And even the local children know that Evil Mary waits in the house for anyone foolish enough to walk through the front door.

Before long, Rosie realizes that her entire life has been defined by the spirit of a woman who died in agony. Can she become the first person to escape Evil Mary, or will she fall victim to the same fate as the house's other occupants?

AMY CROSS

Also by Amy Cross

The Ghosts of Hexley Airport

Ten years ago, more than two hundred people died in a horrific plane crash at Hexley Airport.

Today, some say their ghosts still haunt the terminal building.

When she starts her new job at the airport, working a night shift as part of the security team, Casey assumes the stories about the place can't be true. Even when she has a strange encounter in a deserted part of the departure hall, she's certain that ghosts aren't real.

Soon, however, she's forced to face the truth. Not only is there something haunting the airport's buildings and tarmac, but a sinister force is working behind the scenes to replicate the circumstances of the original accident. And as a snowstorm moves in, Hexley Airport looks set to witness yet another disaster.

AMY CROSS

Also by Amy Cross

The Girl Who Never Came Back

Twenty years ago, Charlotte Abernathy vanished while playing near her family's house. Despite a frantic search, no trace of her was found until a year later, when the little girl turned up on the doorstep with no memory of where she'd been.

Today, Charlotte has put her mysterious ordeal behind her, even though she's never learned where she was during that missing year. However, when her eight-year-old niece vanishes in similar circumstances, a fully-grown Charlotte is forced to make a fresh attempt to uncover the truth.

Originally published in 2013, the fully revised and updated version of *The Girl Who Never Came Back* tells the harrowing story of a woman who thought she could forget her past, and of a little girl caught in the tangled web of a dark family secret.

AMY CROSS

Also by Amy Cross

Asylum
(The Asylum Trilogy book 1)

"No-one ever leaves Lakehurst. The staff, the patients, the ghosts... Once you're here, you're stuck forever."

After shooting her little brother dead, Annie Radford is sent to Lakehurst psychiatric hospital for assessment. Hearing voices in her head, Annie is forced to undergo experimental new treatments devised by a mysterious old man who lives in the hospital's attic. It soon becomes clear that the hospital's staff, led by the vicious Nurse Winter, are hiding something horrific at Lakehurst.

As Annie struggles to survive the hospital, she learns more about Nurse Winter's own story. Once a promising young medical student, Kirsten Winter also heard voices in her head. Voices that traveled a long way to reach her. Voices that have a plan of their own. Voices that will stop at nothing to get what they want.

What kind of signals are being transmitted from the basement of the hospital? Who is the old man in the attic? Why are living human brains kept in jars? And what is the dark secret that lurks at the heart of the hospital?

AMY CROSS

BOOKS BY AMY CROSS

41. The Art of Dying (Detective Laura Foster book 2) (2014)
42. Raven Revivals (Grave Girl book 2) (2014)
43. Arrival on Thaxos (Dead Souls book 1) (2014)
44. Birthright (Dead Souls book 2) (2014)
45. A Man of Ghosts (Dead Souls book 3) (2014)
46. The Haunting of Hardstone Jail (2014)
47. A Very Respectable Woman (2015)
48. Better the Devil (2015)
49. The Haunting of Marshall Heights (2015)
50. Terror at Camp Everbee (The Ward Z Series book 2) (2015)
51. Guided by Evil (Dead Souls book 4) (2015)
52. Child of a Bloodied Hand (Dead Souls book 5) (2015)
53. Promises of the Dead (Dead Souls book 6) (2015)
54. Days 54 to 61 (Mass Extinction Event book 5) (2015)
55. Angels in the Machine (The Robinson Chronicles book 2) (2015)
56. The Curse of Ah-Qal's Tomb (2015)
57. Broken Red (The Broken Trilogy book 3) (2015)
58. The Farm (2015)
59. Fallen Heroes (Detective Laura Foster book 3) (2015)
60. The Haunting of Emily Stone (2015)
61. Cursed Across Time (Dead Souls book 7) (2015)
62. Destiny of the Dead (Dead Souls book 8) (2015)
63. The Death of Jennifer Kazakos (Dead Souls book 9) (2015)
64. Alice Isn't Well (Death Herself book 1) (2015)
65. Annie's Room (2015)
66. The House on Everley Street (Death Herself book 2) (2015)
67. Meds (The Asylum Trilogy book 2) (2015)
68. Take Me to Church (2015)
69. Ascension (Demon's Grail book 1) (2015)
70. The Priest Hole (Nykolas Freeman book 1) (2015)
71. Eli's Town (2015)
72. The Horror of Raven's Briar Orphanage (Dead Souls book 10) (2015)
73. The Witch of Thaxos (Dead Souls book 11) (2015)
74. The Rise of Ashalla (Dead Souls book 12) (2015)
75. Evolution (Demon's Grail book 2) (2015)
76. The Island (The Island book 1) (2015)
77. The Lighthouse (2015)
78. The Cabin (The Cabin Trilogy book 1) (2015)
79. At the Edge of the Forest (2015)
80. The Devil's Hand (2015)
81. The 13th Demon (Demon's Grail book 3) (2016)
82. After the Cabin (The Cabin Trilogy book 2) (2016)
83. The Border: The Complete Series (2016)
84. The Dead Ones (Death Herself book 3) (2016)

217. The Haunting of Quist House (The Rose Files 1) (2021)
218. The Haunting of Crowford Station (The Ghosts of Crowford 11) (2022)
219. The Curse of Rosie Stone (2022)
220. The First Order (The Chronicles of Sister June book 1) (2022)
221. The Second Veil (The Chronicles of Sister June book 2) (2022)
222. The Graves of Crowford Rise (The Ghosts of Crowford 12) (2022)
223. Dead Man: The Resurrection of Morton Kane (2022)
224. The Third Beast (The Chronicles of Sister June book 3) (2022)
225. The Legend of the Crossley Stag (The Ghosts of Crowford 13) (2022)
226. One Star (2022)
227. The Ghost in Room 119 (2022)
228. The Fourth Shadow (The Chronicles of Sister June book 4) (2022)
229. The Soldier Without a Past (Dead Souls book 14) (2022)
230. The Ghosts of Marsh House (2022)
231. Wax: The Complete Series (2022)
232. The Phantom of Crowford Theatre (The Ghosts of Crowford 14) (2022)
233. The Haunting of Hurst House (Mercy Willow book 1) (2022)
234. Blood Rains Down From the Sky (The Deal Trilogy book 3) (2022)
235. The Spirit on Sidle Street (Mercy Willow book 2) (2022)
236. The Ghost of Gower Grange (Mercy Willow book 3) (2022)
237. The Curse of Clute Cottage (Mercy Willow book 4) (2022)
238. The Haunting of Anna Jenkins (Mercy Willow book 5) (2023)
239. The Death of Mercy Willow (Mercy Willow book 6) (2023)
240. Angel (2023)
241. The Eyes of Maddy Park (2023)
242. If You Didn't Like Me Then, You Probably Won't Like Me Now (2023)
243. The Terror of Torfork Tower (Mercy Willow 7) (2023)
244. The Phantom of Payne Priory (Mercy Willow 8) (2023)
245. The Devil on Davis Drive (Mercy Willow 9) (2023)
246. The Haunting of the Ghost of Tom Bell (Mercy Willow 10) (2023)
247. The Other Ghost of Gower Grange (Mercy Willow 11) (2023)
248. The Haunting of Olive Atkins (Mercy Willow 12) (2023)
249. The End of Marcy Willow (Mercy Willow 13) (2023)
250. The Last Haunted House on Mars and Other Stories (2023)

For more information, visit:

www.amycross.com

AMY CROSS